ANNIE'S LOVE

LINDA KAY

authorHOUSE®

AuthorHouse™ LLC
1663 Liberty Drive
Bloomington, IN 47403
www.authorhouse.com
Phone: 1-800-839-8640

Published by AuthorHouse   08/18/2014

ISBN: 978-1-4969-3400-0 (sc)
ISBN: 978-1-4969-3399-7 (e)

Library of Congress Control Number: 2014914703

CONTENTS

ACKNOWLEDGEMENTS

I am forever grateful to my wonderful husband, Jerry, for his patience with me in working to get my writing published. He has spent many hours looking at me from the back, as I'm focused on the computer in front of me. Also a special thanks to my family and friends who have read through the story and helped with some ideas: Jerry, my daughter, Heidi, friend Sue and neighbor Arlene in Illinois, and friend Carol in Georgia. You have all contributed to making my story ready for publishing. Also thanks to the family of AuthorHouse for all their support and guidance.

INTRODUCTION

Annie Ribold was a child of the 60s, a time in history when the generations of teens and parents were vastly separated. Recreational drugs were rampant, the opposition to the war in Vietnam was escalating, and young people were questioning the role of government and parental rules in their lives. They depended on each other for emotional support. Communication among young people was increasing. Parents were not familiar with the language, free love, and struggles among members of this generation. Children wanted answers they had not been allowed to pose in the past. Most parents had never been exposed to any drugs beyond what was prescribed by the doctors. They weren't even aware of the effects of recreational drugs on personalities and behaviors. Many young people were leaving home to join communes and alienating their parents, leaving families torn apart by the generational differences.

With women working away from home, burning bras, and taking on different roles in the family, the perception of what defines a mother began to change. Some of this independence and determination will be revealed in *Annie's Love*.

How do we measure a mother's love? Some might think of the warm, loving woman who bathed, clothed and fed them in their youth. Some will remember the woman who attended every softball game, and cheered for the team from behind the fence. Some will recall the dedicated woman who helped with homework, pushing for those good grades that would eventually secure college acceptance.

But what about those who might have suffered immeasurable sacrifice to give a child some hope? The mothers who gave up on a rebellious child for peace in the home? Some mother may have loved an adopted child as her own. A mother's love comes in many forms, and this book will give readers a better concept of mother love in the changing world of the 60s and 70s, as Jeff Lipton searches for his birth mother and his heritage.

Annie's Love is based on the print by C. Clyde Squires, entitled "Mother Love", one of five prints depicting the various stages of love. These prints are in a frame given to my Grandmother for a shower gift in 1916. The print was handed down to my mother and finally to me. This book is the first product of my imagination, looking at these pictures kept in my family for so many years. My hope is to publish a series of five books, one for each of these beautiful prints.

Chapter 1
ANNIE - 1969

"Come on, Carrie, let's get going!" Annie was anxious to get to the English class she was taking with her roommate, Carrie Bloom. Carrie and Annie Ribold had been friends in high school, and now they had one whole semester of college behind them, active in the party scene at State. Annie was anxious to submit her paper, written in protest to the Vietnam War, and was sure that Professor Hyde would be really pleased with it.

"I'm coming! I couldn't find my gray sweater, and it's pretty cold outside. I can't wear the green one; it clashes with my pants!" Carrie was distraught.

"We are just going to an English class, not a dance!" Annie was losing patience, checking her watch.

"Okay, I'm ready. What's all the rush, anyway? We have a good fifteen minutes to get across campus for the class."

"I want to get this paper turned in, and I want a good seat on the right side of the room, over by the windows. There's a guy in the class that sits over there, and I want to meet him." Annie's eyes sparkled at the prospect of the planned meeting.

"What's his name?" Carrie asked, adjusting her long blonde curls one more time.

"I have no idea. That's why I want to meet him, dummy

!" Carrie and Annie laughed, and rushed out the door, grabbing coats and purses and tossing book bags over their shoulders as they pulled the door shut behind them.

"So describe this guy to me." Carrie was now curious about Annie's interest, and hurried her pace to keep up with Annie, who had been blessed with longer legs.

"He's kind of tall and has dark hair and a gorgeous smile…. Cute butt, too!" I know he has noticed me, because he was watching me one day when I looked over at him. He smiled and winked." Annie rolled her eyes.

"Have you seen him at the frat parties?" Carrie asked, since that's where they had met most of the guys they were seeing.

"Don't think so." Annie bounded up the stairs into the new Carver Hall with Carrie at her heels. They entered the crowded classroom and found seats on the right side of the room, where Annie had hoped to sit, and settled in. Annie made sure to leave an empty seat behind her. The room was bathed in early morning sunshine reflecting off the blackboard at the front. About five minutes later the target of Annie's interest sauntered into the classroom and took the seat. Annie slid down in her chair when she saw him. She felt a shiver as he leaned forward, and she could feel his warm breath on her neck.

"I'll bet your name is Annie Ribold, you're a freshman, and you live in Oaks Hall," he said. She could smell his cologne.

Annie turned around in her chair to face him. "Well now, that's not fair, because I don't know your name." She gave him a coquettish smile and batted her eyes.

Mark extended his right hand. "Mark Moss. Glad to meet you, Annie." Mark had the most incredible smile Annie had ever seen. She felt her interest in him growing. "I'm about to finish up at this place and get on with my life. Want to run away with me?" The flirtation was very obvious.

"Well, you'd have to make it worth my while," she replied, knowing that he was teasing her.

"How 'bout coffee or hot chocolate after class for starters?"

"OK, but I warn you, I'll probably also need a donut, since I haven't had any breakfast." She tossed her long, dark hair behind her, and turned to face the professor.

The English class was probably the longest class Annie could remember. She could feel Mark watching her. After class, she told Carrie she would catch up with her at the dorm, and walked with Mark to the student union. He carried her book bag, and opened doors for her. *Nice guy, expensive shoes, an air of confidence.* She was definitely intrigued by this guy!

"What would you like?" Mark asked her, as he slid her book bag onto a bench in a booth in the far corner of the student union. The room was a din of noisy students visiting at booths, tables and stools positioned by a counter lined with various snack items for sale. The floor was a checkerboard of black and white tile, smudged with tracked snow from shoes.

"I'll have hot chocolate and a donut with sprinkles, thanks," she replied, catching his eyes with hers. "And would you squirt some whipped cream on the hot chocolate?"

"Comin' right up," Mark said, as he sauntered off to the cafeteria line. Annie watched him walk away. His jeans were tight and emphasized firm legs and butt. She looked away to the window facing the quad. It had started to snow, and looked so bleak and cold outside. A picture of her home in winter crossed her mind. Days at home had become so tense with her mom. Her dad just stayed out of her way, but her mom was nagging her all the time about what she was doing at school. At least she only had to see them on holidays, and this Thanksgiving and Christmas had been much too long to be in her home town.

"Looks like the snow is setting in," Mark said as he returned with their drinks and donuts. "I'm free the rest of the day. What's your schedule?"

"This was my only class this morning. I have a biology class this afternoon, but I'm willing to blow it off for a good alternative plan." There was no doubt that she was making her attraction to Mark obvious, and he was well aware. Annie used a spoon to get a dollop of whipped cream and licked it off the spoon slowly. Then she took a sip of the chocolate, getting a bit of whipped cream on the end of her nose. "Oops!" Annie said, as she whisked it away with her finger and offered it to Mark.

Mark licked the whipped cream off her finger. "Um, good stuff!" he said, looking into her eyes. "Tell me, Annie Ribold, just what brings you to State? Are you studying to be an astronaut so you can go to the moon?"

"Hardly that!" Annie replied. "Actually I don't know what I really want to do when I finish. I really hate studying, but my folks are dead set on it, since *they* didn't get a college education. This is my second semester here, and I did okay last term. I've even worked off the 'freshman fifteen', thanks to the aerobics class I'm taking. What about you? You said you are almost done?"

"Just a few more months, and I'm outta here. My degree is in engineering, but I'm not sure how I'll use it.

Tell me more about you, Annie. Where are you from?" Marks eyes were focused on hers.

"I'm from the little town of Green Meadow. I have parents there and one brother, Marty, who is a junior in high school. My parents are really straight and don't understand me. My mom and I don't get along. They are supporting the government and the war and follow all the 'rules', if you know what I mean. I was home for Christmas and thought I'd lose my mind. My roommate Carrie and I have been friends since grade school. She's a great gal, and you'd like her. What's your story?" Annie leaned forward and waited for his response.

"I grew up in an orphanage and don't know who my parents are, or if I have any siblings." Mark looked down at the table and tapped his spoon a couple of times, then he continued. "I grew up in Glenbrook, but I've been living around here since I got out of high school. I work part time, and I make enough to get by with my student aid and scholarships." Another pause. "What do you say we take a drive, and I'll show you my apartment?" Mark picked up his cup, and slid out of the booth.

Annie was stunned. "You grew up in an orphanage? I don't think I've ever known anyone in that situation." She realized that she had been a little insensitive. "I'm sorry, I just was a little surprised at what you told me. Was it really bad?" She felt anxious for Mark, as she envisioned an orphanage from movies she had seen. She began to slide out of the booth.

"No, not really. I had some good friends, and we stuck together. Our sponsors were pretty good to us, and we had plenty to eat and clothes on our backs, although not always the newest or latest fashion. We all learned how to fend for ourselves." Mark tossed their cups in the trash can and took Annie's arm to lead her out of the building. "My car's in the student parking lot."

They walked across the quad to the parking lot, and Mark led her to a shiny new Ford Mustang, opening the door for her to slide into the passenger seat. "Part of my football scholarship package", he lied, not being at college on anyone's scholarship. He switched on the key and the mufflers vibrated. Mark eased out of the parking space and turned toward the exit, stopping only briefly at the guard station. He turned onto the campus main street and then out toward the east side of town. After just five minutes of blacktop they arrived at the converted house used now for student apartments. He parked his car in the designated spot, and opened the car door for Annie to climb out.

"That was quick! Wouldn't it be easier to walk?" Annie teased. She could see that Mark just liked to drive the car, even for that short distance to the campus, and didn't blame him.

When they arrived at Mark's room at the end of the hallway on the second floor, Mark unlocked the door and pushed it open for her to enter. Annie peered inside. It was definitely a guy's apartment. There were some clothes splayed over the back of the couch and several magazines on the coffee table in disarray. On the walls were some posters of scantily dressed pinups, and a couple of football team banners hung near the kitchen doorway. A window was open, and a sheer curtain had been sucked out the window. The cold air made Annie shiver.

Mark tossed his car keys on the end table by the sofa, and walked into the kitchen. "Can I get you a beer?" he asked Annie.

"Sure, if you have one really cold." Annie looked around the room, then out the window, dragged the curtain back into the room and closed it against the brisk January wind. She walked to the couch and sunk into the cushion. The ray of sun that shone in through the window highlighted the dust on the furniture. Annie smiled.

"You have a beautiful smile, Annie". Mark handed her a beer. "What's so amusing?"

"Just noticing how much this place looks like a bachelor pad," said Annie. "Do you entertain girls here often?" She looked at Mark and waited for his response, as he sat down beside her.

"To tell you the truth, my roommate and I don't usually have this place in good enough shape to have any company." He paused, smiling at her. "...let alone beautiful girls. You're seeing it on one of the better days." Mark slowly rolled a joint and lit it. He took a long drag and offered it to Annie. "Want a hit?" he asked.

Annie accepted the joint and took a drag. She held the smoke, and then exhaled. "Mmmmm. I like," she whispered. "Do you always have a supply of pot around the house? Living a bit dangerously perhaps?"

"We don't have any trouble with cops here. We try to keep things quiet and not draw attention. There is plenty more where that came from." Mark took another drag and handed it to Annie. He sat closer to her on the sofa, and put his arm around her. They drank their beers and smoked in silence for a few minutes.

"Want to get more comfortable?" He lifted her chin and kissed her, touching her tongue with his as he parted her lips.

Annie was feeling the effects of the marijuana and the beer. She responded to Mark's kiss, putting her arm around his shoulders and pressing her chest against him. She wore a wool sweater and the scratchy fabric was rubbing against her bare breast. Mark backed away, stood up, and pulled Annie to her feet. He kissed her again, feeling her body against his, and knew that she was aware of his arousal against her. He reached beneath her sweater and cupped her breast in his hand, rubbing the nipple with his thumb. Taking his hand, she followed him into the bedroom, where the bed was still unmade from the night before. They stood together beside the bed and kissed again, passionately.

Mark stripped off her sweater, then removed his own sweater and pulled her against him. She made no sound as he leaned her back onto the bed and began to unzip her jeans. As he tugged at her jeans, he kissed her breasts and felt her arch her body toward him. She unbuckled his belt, unbuttoned the button at the waistline, and then unzipped his jeans, reaching inside. Mark stood up to get rid of his jeans, while Annie slipped out of her panties. She turned and reached into the top drawer of the bedside table, and as she expected, found a condom. She took it from the package and helped Mark put it on.

Her touch was almost more than Mark could bear. He pushed her back onto the bed, and ran his hand inside her thigh, feeling her dampness. Rolling on top of her he lay between her thighs. Annie welcomed him, arching her body up to meet his every thrust. He kissed her with passion and watched her face as she released sounds of satisfaction, digging her fingernails into his back. His thrust stopped with his own release. He kissed her again. "You are one hot woman!" he said, as he rolled away from her.

Annie turned on her side against him. "Not so bad yourself!" she teased. "I'll bet you say that to all your girls."

Mark kissed her on the tip of her nose. "Annie, we are going to have some great time together, I can tell that for sure. You could be more addictive than any drug we could find." Mark got up from the bed, grabbed his clothes, and went into the bathroom. He came back out with only his jeans on and sat on the edge of the bed, fondling her breast. "Can I keep you here, just like this for a while?"

"I've got all afternoon," Annie replied. Standing, she slipped into Mark's shirt hanging behind the bathroom door. She didn't bother with any other unnecessary clothing.

When Mark finally took her back to her dorm hours later, she tip-toed into her dorm room, and quickly fell asleep on her bed. The rest of the world could just pass her by. Mark Moss was all that was on her mind, among the dreams of an exciting future together. She could not know of the turmoil ahead for the two of them, nor of the child who would steal her heart.

Chapter 2
JEFF'S SEARCH BEGINS

Jeff Lipton sat in the tall grass around the tombstone and read the inscription. Florence Ann Ribold Moss; June 1, 1950 - May 10, 1974. A brisk October wind whistled through the tall oak trees that lined the cemetery fence. Dry leaves painted in vibrant fall colors whirled and scattered among the tombstones, and a pungent odor filled the air as some leaves burned in carefully raked piles along the roadway. Clouds obscured the sun, creating an eerie sense of gloom that settled into the late morning.

Had it come to this? To find that his birth mother had died so many years before, buried in a tiny cemetery in Iowa among other deceased members of her family (and his)? He suddenly felt overwhelmed. Was his grief in knowing that his mother was dead, or was it in now having come to what might be the end of his quest? Jeff reached out and touched the inscription, deeply etched in the cold granite, as though it would give him some sense of kinship.

Jeff felt the pain of the headache that had been increasing in intensity. It wasn't so difficult to track her to this place. So why hadn't someone tried to find him? He'd rest tonight, and tomorrow he would see what he could find out about Florence Ann Ribold Moss in the little town of Green Meadow.

Jeff walked back to his red Impala, turned the key to bring the engine to life, and backed down the gravel lane to the main blacktop into town. Unnoticed by him, an elderly figure carried a handful of fall flowers across the monuments toward the grave Jeff had just left behind.

George and Sue Lipton had always been open with Jeff about his adoption. Jeff could vaguely remember his birth mother, although after so many years, the image had faded into obscurity. Even the picture he had of her didn't help much. The Liptons, who had adopted him at the age of four, had told him only that her name was Florence Ann "Annie" Moss. As with many adoptive children, Jeff felt a nagging to find his birth parents, to connect to the family lineage.

The road back into Green Meadow was just two lanes, and Jeff was delayed by a large harvesting machine, moving along at a snail's pace with nowhere to pass. Jeff was in no hurry, as he was consumed with his own thoughts and questions. The farmer soon waved him on, and he was finally able to pass the behemoth machine. The harvested fields looked dry and stripped naked of their crops. He raised a hand to thank the driver for the help in passing, as he pulled back in front of him.

Jeff drove the remaining distance to the only motel in town, where he hoped to spend the night. The office had a neon sign reading "Vacancy".

"How can I help you?" Jeff noticed a slight limp in the man's gait, as he moved to the counter from a nearby desk. His glasses were perched on the end of his nose so that Jeff thought they might fall off when he looked down at the registration book. An unruly wisp of hair tumbled onto his forehead.

"I need a room with just one bed for a couple of nights," Jeff answered. "I have some work in town, and I'm not sure yet how long I'll be staying." His mind raced ahead to where he would need to go to find more information on Annie.

"Not a problem. This time of year we don't have a full house. You'll find the rooms comfortable. There's Peggy's Diner just a block to the east, and a new Quick Mart next to Mike's Service Station on Highway 150. Room's $49.95 a night plus tax. And you can stay as long as you want. Anything I can help you with, just give me a buzz." He looked up and smiled at Jeff.

"How will you be paying for the room? We take cash, check or credit card." The handsome customer before him was dressed in a casual shirt and jeans, wore a brown leather flight jacket, and his dark hair curled out from under his Cardinals' baseball cap. Tanned and buff, tall and slender, two deep dimples were revealed in his cheeks when he smiled. "You look familiar. Do I know you from somewhere?" he asked Jeff.

Jeff handed over the credit card for inspection. "Not that I know of," he replied.

The clerk pressed the card down into the credit card machine, and placed the bank document over it to get the imprint. Jeff watched as he made the call to get the approval on the card. There was an easy manner about the man. He was dressed in a crisp white shirt and black slacks, and wore wing-tipped dress shoes.

"OK, got it!" The approval was issued. He checked his log for the rooms available, and then turned to retrieve the key from the grid behind his desk, narrowly missing the Coke he had placed on the corner.

"Room's Number 12.... just out the door, turn to your left, and down to the third door. You can park your car right out in front of the room. Have a good stay with us, and remember to let me know if there is any way I can be of assistance. Name's Al. I've lived in this area for about thirty years, so I know the town pretty well."

"Thanks, Al." Jeff had no intention of getting into a conversation with Al today. The events of the morning were overwhelming, and his head was throbbing. He walked out the front door to his car and made a fast run to the Quick Mart for some aspirin before entering the room.

Al was right; the room wasn't state-of-the-art. The heater in the room was mounted on the wall, with the fan running at full blast. The air felt a bit clammy and cold, so Jeff went straight to the dials on the heater to regulate the fan and the temperature. *Geez! It's freezing in here!* Jeff muttered to himself.

There were heavy, flowery drapes over sheer curtains on the windows that looked out onto the lake behind the motel. Jeff opened both sets to get a good look at the water. The lake sparkled in the midday sun that had peeked through the clouds, and reflected the trees that shaded the distant shore. A pair of ducks swam lazily beneath the overhanging oak tree limbs. On the far right, an older man was fishing from the bank. His straw hat was losing its weave on one side, and sported a fishing lure on the other. Jeff wondered if he would ever catch anything.

A small pier jutted out into the lake from the bank behind the motel. Jeff thought he might take a walk out on the stepping stones to the pier later and enjoy the view from a better perspective. But for now, he just wanted to lay back and rest his eyes. He found an ice machine in an alcove between two other rooms, retrieved the ice in the bucket provided, and returned to the room.

The bathroom counter held a tray with a bottle of shampoo, a packet of lotion, and four glasses, wrapped in their cellophane envelopes. Jeff opened one of the wrappers, filled a glass with water from the tap, and downed two capsules. Then he set the alarm on the clock radio for 4:30 and stretched out on top of the coverlet. Where would he start to find the missing pieces to help him understand Annie? What was she like?

Bzzzz....Bzzzz....Bzzzz.... The clock radio alarm sounded, waking Jeff from a sound sleep. He sat straight up, rubbed his eyes, and for a couple of seconds couldn't remember where he was or what he was doing there. What time of day was it? Jeff looked at the clock and noted the time at 4:30 PM. The headache seemed to have gone, and his head was clearing. Annie Moss. His mother. His search to find his birth mother had brought him to this small town of some 2,000 people. It had been pretty simple to find her. He recalled the conversation with his parents.

"Jeff, if this is what you want to do, I will be happy to help you. The last we saw of Annie was when she signed the papers 30 years ago." Sue Lipton had some anxiety in her voice as she shared this with Jeff. It had all started the evening before, as they were eating dinner. Even though Jeff had his own apartment, he often had dinner with his parents. George had been a bit late getting home from work, and they were eating a late dinner, just George, Jeff and Sue.

"What have you been up to today, Jeff?" George had asked.

"I went to work this morning, and spent some time in the library this afternoon, doing some research for a project I am working on. I ran into a friend from college, and found out that his parents are getting a divorce. He mentioned that he was sort of feeling like an orphan." Jeff paused for a moment, and continued. "It got me to thinking about you and mom and me, and about my adoption. I hadn't thought about it for some time. I don't want to hurt you and Mom, but I would like to try to find out about my birth family. How do you feel about that? Would you help me?"

Sue drew in a quick breath, trying not to show alarm at Jeff's request. George was the first to answer. He laid down his fork, and picked up his napkin, holding it tightly in his hand. "We told you long ago that you were adopted and how much we love you. I think we have always known that this day would come, when you would want to find out about your natural family. Your mother and I want you to be happy and content in your life. You should be able to know your own mind."

"I have a copy of the adoption papers with your mother's signature," Sue responded. "The circumstances that led up to the adoption were very unusual, but we were happy to be given the opportunity." Sue's voice was a bit shaky, but she continued.

Jeff was alarmed. "You have never told me any of this before. Why not? How did you know where I was born and when I was born?"

"The time just had not been right for us to talk to you about this, Jeff," George said. "We were given your birth certificate, which shows your date of birth and the hospital in which you were born. Your father is not listed on the birth certificate, only Annie Moss. We know she loved you very much, Jeff."

Jeff calmed down, but remained agitated. "But how can you walk away from a four-year-old child, if you love him?" The question would haunt him until he could get some answers.

"Jeff, you may never know the answer to that question. Tomorrow morning I'll get out the adoption papers for you to see her name and signature, and you can do what you can to find the answers you are looking for. If there is anything we can do to help you, we will. Just remember that we have loved you since the first day we set eyes on you. I think your mother knew that we would take good care of you." Sue's heart was heavy at the prospect of Jeff beginning this search for his family.

She had given Jeff a copy of the adoption papers, along with a picture of him as a newborn, then at about two, and again at three and a half years of age, wearing a cowboy hat and western shirt. Also, within the envelope were a picture of Annie and a picture of an older couple. Sue said that Annie had asked that these not be given to Jeff until he was ready to see them. There were no names written or dates to indicate an age of the people in the pictures.

Florence Ann Moss. The last name had been pretty common and came up on many searches at the library for Jeff, but the first name was a bit unusual. Jeff wondered if she had been named after someone in her family. Finally, he searched records for obituaries in the state, going back year by year. It appeared in a death announcement in a newspaper from the county seat near Green Meadow.

> **Florence Ann Ribold Moss. Died May 10th, 1974. She is survived by her parents, Don and Arlene Ribold of Green Meadow. Gravesite rites will be at the Green Meadow cemetery on May 15th at 10 AM.**

Jeff was astonished and angry. So quickly after getting the name of his birth mother, he had found that she was dead! It was all so surreal. Who were Don and

Arlene Ribold? Why didn't they stay in touch with their grandson? Where were they now? And where was this town Green Meadow? It was all so mysterious.

Jeff shared what he had found with George and Sue. "I have to find this place and see the cemetery for myself. There have to be more answers. I've found Green Meadow on the map, and I'm going there Friday to see what I can find."

"Do you want us to go with you?" George asked his son.

"No, I have to do this on my own," said Jeff. "It will only take me an hour or so to drive there, and I'll plan to spend a couple of nights somewhere in the area. I took off Friday and Monday from work."

Sue was concerned. "Just keep in touch with us, okay?"

"I will. I can call from where I'm staying." Jeff was determined to be free to do his searching. The prospect of finding someone, anyone, who knew Annie Moss, gave him hope.

Now he was here, right here in Green Meadow. He had seen her grave. There couldn't be another Florence Ann Moss. And Ribold had been her maiden name. The obituary had listed her parents as survivors. Were they still in Green Meadow? Did they know that he existed? Jeff dialed 9 for an outside line, and then dialed his parents' number. Sue answered the phone.

"Hello?" Sue's voice was, as always, cheerful.

"Hi, Mom," Jeff answered. "I've found the cemetery and Annie's grave. Her maiden name is included in the inscription on the marker. I haven't had a chance to start looking around and asking questions yet, but I'm going to go grab a bite to eat at the local diner."

"Thanks for calling, Jeff. Just let us know how things are going. Love you!"

Jeff hung up the phone. He picked out some clean clothes and decided to get a quick shower before heading out for dinner at Peggy's Diner. Outside, the weather had deteriorated, and a brisk wind was whistling at the window of the motel. The water in the lake outside was whipped by the wind, and it had grown darker, reflecting the street lights on the opposite side of the lake. The fisherman had gone, and the ducks were hiding somewhere among the grasses. Jeff would be lucky if he could eat dinner and get back to the motel before it started to rain.

Peggy's Diner was obviously the local gathering place for the town. Toward the back of the restaurant was a large round table with an assortment of town folks enjoying a cup of coffee and chatting about all the latest events in the world.

All eyes were on Jeff as he walked into the restaurant. A waitress motioned to him to take any empty seat. He decided on a booth, and slid onto the bench facing the door. The waitress was quick to arrive at his table.

"I'm Carol, and I'll be takin' care of you. What can I get you to drink?" She handed him a menu. Carol was about 5'5", Jeff was guessing. She had long, straight blonde hair and the bluest eyes Jeff had ever seen. She wore an apron with a Peggy's Diner emblem on the front, and pockets to hold her ticket book and straws.

"Just a Coke with lots of ice would be fine, thanks. Is there a special for the day?" *Sometimes these are the best meals.*

"It's Friday night, so we have fried walleye fillets, all you can eat, French fries, and a salad. Or you can order anything from the menu." Carol was ready with pen in hand to take an order.

"Ok, I'll check out the menu and be ready when you come back." He wasn't sure fish was what he wanted to eat. He watched her stroll back behind the counter to get his drink. From what Jeff could surmise considering the apron, she had a figure to die for, and he wondered why she would be working in this diner. She looked to be in her late 20s. Maybe she was commuting to school at the university?

Carol was back to his booth quickly with his Coke. "Are you ready to order?" she asked. She had out her ticket book, pencil poised to write. Her hands looked soft, and her nails were carefully manicured. "You're a stranger in town, aren't you? I don't recall seeing you here before."

"Yes, I'm a stranger to Green Meadow, and I'll have the walleye dinner." Jeff caught her glance as she looked up at his response. Those eyes sparkled with mischief, and Jeff had to look back down at the menu. "And could you bring me some onion rings as well?"

"Sure thing. I'll just bring them out with your meal, if that's Ok. It's a good little town, by the way, and I hope you enjoy your stay here. There's not much to do, though. I'll get this order in. Let me know if you need a refill on your Coke." Carol again walked behind the counter and delivered her ticket to the clothespin line that had been strung up above the serving window from the kitchen area. "Order!" she hollered to the cook beyond the window. Then she sauntered off to wait on another couple who had seated themselves at the booth behind Jeff. Jeff could feel her glancing at him. He was suddenly glad he had taken that nap and changed clothes, so he was up for her inspection.

Carol was back quickly with his salad and a basket of crackers wrapped in cellophane. "Your order will be up soon, so I'll bring it out as soon as it hits the counter." Carol smiled at him. "Enjoy your salad."

Jeff poured out the dressing on his salad, and noticed that the lettuce was shredded fine just the way he liked it. He looked out the front windows of the restaurant and saw the city office across the street, wondering if he might be able to get some information there. An office for the local paper must be somewhere on the main street. Another possibility might be the library. In any case, he would have until Monday afternoon to see what he could find out here in Green Meadow before he had to get back to Aubrey and his job.

Jeff thought briefly about his job, remembering his conversations with Gary. He had worked for Gary Olsen practically all through high school, working after school and in the summer at the car dealership. When Jeff had finished his studies at Iowa State in accounting, Gary had offered him a job and eventual partnership in the business. "I know it's not the best job you could find, but you will have some opportunity here to get into the business and learn a good deal about how things operate. If you are interested, I'll have my attorney draw up an agreement for you to earn interest in the dealership. I need help with the accounting, the ordering, and the personnel issues. It's just gotten to be too much for one person."

Jeff had considered the fact that he would be close to his folks and that his living expenses wouldn't be too high, living in a smaller community. Gary was offering him a chance to be in business for himself someday, and Jeff really liked the idea. Gary was already taking off more time to travel with his wife, leaving Jeff in charge. Because of that, Jeff felt he was due a couple of days off himself.

"Here's your walleye order, and your onion rings…. Er,… what did you say your name is?" Carol was back at his booth.

"I didn't say what my name is, but my name's Jeff." Jeff smiled at her interest in him. "I only need a cup of black coffee at this point, if you could bring that to me."

"I'll be back in a flash," Carol responded, her eyes sparkling. She returned quickly with the coffee. "Anything else I can get you?" she asked.

"Just maybe sit with me a couple of minutes when you are finished with your shift, so I can ask you a few questions about Green Meadow." Jeff was hoping she would be off work soon.

"My shift is over at 7, if you'd like to hang around. I'll keep filling up your coffee cup. And the men's room is in the back, if you need it." Carol grinned at him.

"Very funny," Jeff replied. "But thanks for the tip. And I'll eat slowly."

There was something about Jeff that made her want to know him a little better. He was handsome and had those dimples in the hollows of his cheeks when he smiled. She was curious about what brought him to Green Meadow, if he didn't know much about the town. Why would he be interested in this place?

He again watched her walk back around the end of the counter and back to the coffee and soda bar to get refills for other customers. There was a spring in her step, and he sensed that she was interested in talking with him.

After several cups of coffee, and just one trip to the men's room, Jeff noticed that it was a few minutes after seven by his watch. And right on cue, Carol sat down on the bench across the booth from him. "Whew! It feels good to sit down and get the weight off. By the way, I'm Carol Braun." She extended her hand as a greeting.

"And I'm Jeff Lipton." Jeff smiled as he took her hand in his. Her hands were warm and soft, her handshake firm.

"So tell me what brings you to Green Meadow?" Carol looked at him with those dancing blue eyes, resting her chin on her palms, elbows on the table. She had taken off her work apron, and her sweater revealed the voluptuous figure Jeff had already imagined.

"It's kind of a long story, actually. I'm here to do a bit of family research. I was adopted, and have recently found information about my birth mother. I traced her here to Green Meadow, but unfortunately, she is deceased. So now I'm trying to track down other family members. I thought maybe you might be able to tell me where to go to get information on local people." Jeff felt comfortable sharing his situation with Carol.

"Wow! That's heavy! I'm sorry that you weren't able to have a happy reunion with your birth mother. Who was she? Do I know her?" Carol was anxious to help.

"I doubt if you knew her. Her name was Annie Moss, Annie Ribold Moss. And she died in 1975 at the age of about 25. I'm guessing that her parents also lived here at the time, so I'd like to find them as well," Jeff continued.

"No, I don't know the name. My family moved me here about 15 years ago, and I graduated from high school here. I'm going to Iowa State, but took a semester off to earn some money and help my mom. It's kind of taking me a long time to get through, but it will be worth it in the long run. I'll bet I can tell you some places to go for answers about local folks. In fact, in here on Saturday morning lots of the locals meet for breakfast. Someone will surely know how to help you get some facts together." Carol was intrigued by Jeff. "Tell you what, let's drive around town a bit, and I'll show you some of the store buildings and churches where you might also get some information. I'll even drive."

"It's a deal. You can tell me more about your studies at State while we are driving. I appreciate the offer." Jeff felt a burden being lifted from his shoulders, just having someone to share his challenge. "I'll just pay this bill, and we can go."

Jeff took out his wallet and handed his ticket and the cash to the cashier. He handed Carol a tip for the meal and said, "Somehow I feel this isn't nearly enough."

She took the tip. "Oh, forget it. It's kind of overcast outside and threatening rain, but we can still get a look at the town." She smiled and opened the restaurant door. "After you, Jeff Lipton."

Chapter 3
ANNIE, SPRING, 1969

The next several months went by quickly for Annie, as she spent most of her time with Mark. In fact, she was at Mark's more than she was in her dorm room with Carrie. Carrie was understanding, and told Annie that she would do the same thing if she had half the chance. Sometimes Mark's roommate was at the apartment, but they had it to themselves much of the time. Annie had introduced Ronnie to Carrie, and they were hitting it off pretty well.

Mark had introduced Annie to some stronger drugs and continued to supply her with all the marijuana and beer she wanted. Annie loved him so much, and she knew that Mark loved her, too. He was very mysterious about where he had obtained the drugs, and he always had a lot of money. She decided that she really didn't want to know what was going on. Her life was more full and exciting than she could have ever hoped it could be, and she didn't want anything to ruin the relationship.

Annie managed to attend most of her classes, but her grades had fallen to barely passing. She knew her parents would be furious with her. Mark was graduating, and Annie was faced with going home for the summer. One late spring evening, as they were walking in the park near the lake, Mark held her hand tightly. He turned her toward him and kissed her.

"I'm going to be done with school in a couple of weeks, and I'm moving to New York State, a town called Wahlberg. I want you to go with me." Mark looked in her eyes. "We can find a place, and you can go to school if you want to. I've got a job lined up there and we'll have enough money for us to live on. I don't want to go without you."

Annie looked at him and swallowed hard. The past several months had been one big party with Mark. He looked so serious now. She couldn't bear the thought of being away from him. But she knew her parents would never let her go with him willingly. "What will I tell my mom and dad?" Annie didn't know where to begin, but she knew she was not anxious to present this idea.

"Annie, there is no way your folks are going to just let you go. If you go with me, you'll have to just tell them you are going. We'll have a great time together. I know there is going to be a huge party out in New York in August, and I want you to be there with me. There's going to be music and a really neat, peaceful gathering of young people like you and me. It'll be so cool." Mark was pleading with Annie to go with him.

The prospect of running away with Mark gave Annie a thrill, but at the same time, she knew she would not be able to look back. Her parents would go nuts when she told them. Maybe she would just write a letter. Or maybe she would get high and then call them, so she would be a little braver. And when would she tell them? They would be looking for her to come home from college as soon as finals were over. There was no way she could go home at all, or they would never let her leave. Annie knew she had to go with Mark.

"You're going to do what?" shrieked Carrie. "Annie, you can't just go away like that with Mark. What will you tell your parents? They will freak out!" Carrie sat down on the side of her bed and looked at Annie. She could see by the gleam in her eyes that Annie was determined to be with Mark. "Is it possible that you could just get married, and your folks would accept Mark that way?"

"He hasn't asked me to marry him, Carrie, just go away with him. I couldn't stand to be away from him. I love him!" Annie was close to tears, but held on to her resolve. She walked to the window of the dorm and looked out at the spring day. "You have to keep the secret for me. I'll keep in touch, but you can't tell my parents where I am. They will send someone to find me for sure, and make me go back to school, or even worse, back to Green Meadow." The prospect of having to be under her parents' control, living by all those rules and worrying about what the neighbors thought was unimaginable to Annie.

"If you go, then don't tell me where you are. You can call me sometimes to talk, but I don't want to have to lie about where you are. It's better if I don't know, so I can say I don't know. How are you going to tell them?" Carrie was still trying to get a grip on the scene that was unfolding before her. "What about school? Aren't you planning to finish?"

"You know how much I hate being in school. Besides, Mark will take care of me. He's going to get a job that will provide for us. We'll have complete freedom to go where we want, party when we want, and have an exciting life together. You'll see!" Annie had convinced herself that Mark would continue to offer her fun and excitement. She didn't need her family, if she could have Mark.

"Annie, you have completely lost it. But you are my best friend, and I love you. Your secret will be safe with me. Just let me know when you are leaving, and tell me good-bye." Carrie hugged her.

Carrie wasn't crazy about being in school either, but there was no way she would be able to walk away from her mom. They had been through so much together, and she knew that her mom would only want her to be happy. Carrie knew that Annie didn't have the same relationship with Arlene. Annie seemed to be resistant to anything Arlene offered or suggested, and they were constantly at odds. Carrie wondered if Annie had become addicted to the drugs she and Mark shared, but she didn't have a solution for that, for sure. There was something vindictive in the way that Annie looked at leaving her family for Mark.

Annie had told her parents about Mark when she was home for the Easter holiday. She told them that he was an engineering student, but told them no details about his background, definitely not anything about his background.

"What do you know about this boy, Annie?" Arlene had asked. "Have you been seeing him very long?" It seemed like a pretty simple question to Arlene.

"Mom, stop!" Annie was defensive immediately. "He's just a friend, and I see him when we have school parties and outings. I don't need to know his life history at this point, and certainly, neither do you." Annie had stomped out of the living room, leaving Arlene with her mouth open. Annie's surly attitude and belligerence had gotten worse with this year of college. Arlene was at a loss as to what to do about it. She ached inside for the daughter she had once known, who would bring light into a room just by walking into it. What had happened? Arlene had followed her into the kitchen.

"Annie, what is wrong with you? I can't say anything to you without you getting upset and yelling at me. We had always had such good times together, and lately things are so different. Is there anything I can do?" Arlene wanted to offer Annie a chance to calm down and talk to her.

"Just leave me alone, Mom. That's all I ask. I'm going back to school tomorrow after dinner, and I just want a peaceful day." Annie shrugged her shoulders as though that would be as simple a request as she could offer. "I don't want to talk about school, or Mark, or anything else in my life with you, so just stop nagging at me!" Annie had walked away from Arlene and gone up the stairs to her room, leaving her mother with tears welling in her eyes.

Arlene had called her friend Sandy to talk to her. Between them they considered the possibility of Annie being involved in the drug scene at college. Arlene was so unfamiliar with any signs of drug use, and she felt totally helpless as to where to begin to determine if Annie was using drugs. After talking with Sandy, Arlene had gone to the library to look up some information. What she read was very frightening to her. Articles indicated that drugs were readily available on college campuses, and that many students were smoking marijuana and using LSD, a hallucinogenic drug. There was reference to the fact that in many young people, the drugs produced extreme changes in behavior. Arlene copied some information to share with Don.

Don read through the articles Arlene had copied for him. "Let's make some plans for this summer to get Annie away from Green Meadow and take a trip, where she won't have access to any drugs. We can see if it makes a difference in her personality. And we can check her room to see if we find any evidence of drugs as well. If nothing else, we will get her to a doctor to see if we can prove she is or is not using the stuff. School will be over in a couple of months, so we will have a much better chance of dealing with this when she is home for the summer." Arlene and Don felt that at least they had a plan to deal with Annie's bizarre behavior.

Don and Arlene were also pretty caught up in the events of Annie's brother Marty's life at the moment. Marty was a junior in high school, and he was doing extremely well in school and in school sports. The recent awards banquet had been a joy to attend, as Marty received several honors for his junior year. He was still working with Jim Jarrett, earning his own money and saving for college, although there was a good chance that he would get a scholarship in basketball, and possibly some for academics as well. Where Annie seemed to bring constant frustration, Marty provided them with a sense of pride in their son's accomplishments.

Annie finished her beer and took one last drag from the joint. Mark stood beside her while she dialed the number. "Mom, it's Annie," she began. "I'm just calling to tell you that I'm not coming home for the summer, because I'm leaving school with Mark. Don't ask any questions. I'll call you to let you know how I am." Annie paused for the inevitable response.

"What? Annie, what are you doing? You can't just take off with this guy! How will we get hold of you?" Arlene's voice was filled with anger, shock and frustration.

"I told you, no questions. I'll be in touch." Annie was about to hang up the phone.

"Young lady, if you do this, don't bother to come to us for help with school or anything else, for that matter!" Arlene was trembling with the delivery of her ultimatum and realized she was shouting at Annie. Her plans with Don to deal with Annie over the summer raced through her mind.

"Well, don't you worry, Mom," Annie shouted into the phone. "You don't have to be concerned about ever hearing from me again!" Tears streamed down Annie's cheeks as she slammed the phone onto the cradle. She turned to Mark.

"She doesn't care about me at all, just wants me to follow her rules and be the person she wants me to be," she said as she put her arms around him and buried her head in his chest. Mark felt her sob against him, and rubbed her shoulders. For a moment, he felt that he had demanded too much from Annie. Having no family of his own, he had no concept of the dynamics of family relationships. But Annie soon reassured him.

"Let's go. I want us to get on with our life together, and I don't need those people in Green Meadow to be happy. All I need is you." Annie wiped her tears away on her sleeve, and Mark handed her his hanky. Annie's clothes and luggage were already loaded into Mark's car. She had taken out all the money left in her bank account in cash and had it stowed away in her suitcase. Mark had never asked her for money, but Annie felt reassured that she had at least a little money of her own. She had said good-bye to Carrie, not revealing where they were going. Actually, she didn't know exactly where they were going, except it was somewhere in New York, many miles away from Iowa.

Annie and Mark climbed into his car and pulled onto the highway. They would drive all day today, stop somewhere along the way tonight, and then drive the rest of the way tomorrow. In New York they would begin the rest of their life together, Annie Ribold and Mark Moss.

Chapter 4
JEFF'S SEARCH CONTINUES

Jeff woke up and looked at the clock on the nightstand. The dial showed 8 AM. It was Saturday morning. Carol Braun had taken him for a drive around Green Meadow last night to show him where some of the city buildings were located, as well as to point out some of the nicer areas of town with the bigger houses and bigger yards. Carol had been a godsend. It was good to have someone to talk to, and Carol seemed to be genuinely interested in his challenges. He loved her blonde hair and blue eyes, and her obvious independence. She had dropped him off at his car at the diner and had invited him to come to the restaurant today. There were several of the local folks who met at Peggy's on Saturday morning for coffee and breakfast, and Carol thought someone there might know more about the Ribold family. Jeff jumped out of bed, into the shower, dressed quickly, and drove to Peggy's.

"Greetings, stranger!" Carol saw him enter the restaurant. "Come on down here to the round table and have a seat among these local yokels, so they get a chance to meet you." Carol grabbed a mug, filled it with coffee, and met Jeff at the table with it. She handed him a menu as well. "Introduce yourself to these fine folks, and I'll be back to get your order in a few minutes."

Jeff looked at the faces around the table, all looking to him for an introduction. After all, he was the stranger. "I'm Jeff Lipton, from Aubrey. I'm pleased to meet all of you here in Green Meadow." Jeff smiled, and waited for them to make introductions around the table. He knew he would never remember all the names. He gave his order to Carol and joined the conversation. The conglomeration of local folks quickly ignored the fact that Jeff was a stranger, and launched into the typical Saturday morning discussions of politics and gossip. Jeff joined in when he was invited to respond, and he was really enjoying the camaraderie. All of the names of the people mentioned in the conversation from around town were unknown to him.

Carol brought his order. He didn't know when he had eaten such a hardy breakfast, usually eating just a piece of toast or a bowl of cereal on his way out the door to go to work. And he must have had at least three cups of strong coffee before all the plates were cleared away and his ticket was delivered.

Carol brought up the question, speaking matter-of-fact. "Does anyone here remember an Annie Ribold, or her parents, Don and Arlene Ribold? Jeff's looking for some information on them." Jeff caught his breath, waiting for someone to comment. Carol left them to their conversation.

The fellow with the seed company cap, Jeff couldn't remember his name, said, "I remember Don Ribold. He worked for the insurance company here in town. His kid used to work for Jim Jarrett at the grocery store after school and in the summer, I'm sure of it. His wife worked at the paper plant in Staley, if I remember right. They moved away from here probably at least twenty-five or so years ago. But I don't remember an Annie." He looked to his table companions for other thoughts. "Anybody know where they went?"

"Arlene was really active at First Baptist when they lived here. She was good friends with Sandy Stahl. They worked together at the plant. I think Annie was the same age as Sandy's boy, Andy, and they graduated from here in Green Meadow. Sandy and her husband moved to Staley some time ago, but I'm not sure where the Ribold's moved to." Judy contributed a couple of memories.

Ron, leaning back in his chair, was the next to comment. "My daughter was in school when Annie and that boy, Andy, were in high school. She always said Annie was a little wild, kind of hung out with some of the older crowd. She went off to college and didn't come around much after that. Annie's buried out at the cemetery. She died pretty young, and Don and Arlene were pretty torn up about it, but I don't know how she died. Didn't they move to Chatsworth? I bet they would know at the post office, or maybe there's a record at the city building."

Joe listened to all the others. He was curious. "Why are you looking for them, Jeff?"

"I am working on some family history, and just trying to put the missing pieces together. My mother thinks that we are related to the Ribolds." Jeff didn't want to get into any details about his search.

"I'll bet it's been nearly 30 years since the Ribolds buried their daughter out at Prairie Rest." Joe took a sip of his coffee. "No one ever knew the story about her death, only that she had been out of touch with her family for some time. From what I was told, Annie was one of those 'flower children', and she and her parents really clashed. After the boy graduated from college, the whole family up and disappeared from Green Meadow. I think you are right, Ron, that they moved to Chatsworth. But I don't know of anyone who kept in touch with them. Seems like a sad story, for sure." Joe watched Jeff's face to see his reaction. Jeff was looking down at a small notebook, taking down some names, and did not catch his eye. Suzy, reminiscing, said, "I'll probably never know how much my kids experimented with all that drug stuff. Remember the rock music event? It was all over the papers, along with all the Vietnam War protests. It was really a rough time to be a teenager."

"Well, it's not any better now," chimed in Clyde, who was still finishing up his breakfast. "I had an insurance policy that Don sold me at one time. He did move away, but the policy stayed with the company here in town. That kid of Don's, Marty I think his name was, really worked hard down at the grocery store. He graduated from some college in New York and went on to work somewhere, but I have no idea where that might be. We may not have been much help to you, Jeff."

"Everything you can remember is helpful," replied Jeff. "I can take this information to the local library, the local paper, and the city hall to see what else I can find out. I'd really like to find the Ribolds to see if there is a family connection. It sounds like they have had their share of tragedy." Jeff didn't want to talk about them anymore at this point. He felt that he had just uncovered the tip of the iceberg, and that he was going to have to spend some serious time researching Annie and her family. Jeff felt a heaviness enveloping him.

Jeff's table companions started to leave, one by one. Carol had kept Jeff's coffee cup full, so he had no idea how many cups of coffee he might have downed by now. Each of the new acquaintances wished Jeff good luck in his research, and hoped to see him again.

Finally, Carol sat down beside Jeff at his now empty table.

"Well, did you learn anything?" she queried.

"I learned that there are more questions now than when I started," he replied, sighing and giving her a quirky smile.

"I'll just be a few minutes to get some things put away, and I can take you around to some of the resources you have here in town. You can tell me what you have found out." Carol pushed in her chair as she walked back behind the counter, taking the last of the remaining breakfast dishes and Jeff's coffee cup from the table. Jeff put a tip on the table for Carol and walked to the cash register to pay for his breakfast. Then he sat on a chair near the front window to wait for Carol to finish. He watched her work efficiently at bussing the dishes, cleaning coffee pots, and tidying up the work area. But his mind was far away from Peggy's Diner.

"Ready-0? Let's Go!" Carol walked up to Jeff with her purse in hand, ready to walk out the door. She grabbed Jeff by the elbow and pulled him to his feet, then pushed him out the door ahead of her. "My car's at the far end of the parking lot," she said, leaving Jeff with no question that Carol was in charge of escorting him around town this morning. Jeff walked along obediently and climbed into Carol's car. "Okay, Mr. Lipton, where do you want to go first?"

"Let's go first to the newspaper office. One of my table mates thought it would be open this morning, so we might be able to catch someone there. Actually, any office in town is only open in the morning on Saturdays, so we will just have to do the best we can." Jeff found himself to be a little apprehensive about the prospects of what he might learn at the newspaper office. But he felt an unmistakable urge to continue.

Carol drove to the middle of the block, pulled her car into the vertical parking space in front of the newspaper office, and they both got out of the car. Jeff opened the door with the heavy latch, and followed Carol into the large front room. Inside, a desk faced the front of the building, where stacks of newspapers lay haphazardly everywhere, many of them faded with age. Near the front window more recent stacks of papers, obviously sorted and bundled, awaited mailing or delivery to the current week's subscribers. Several large, very old machines lined the walls, and an odor of ink and paper permeated the air. On the walls hung pictures of events in simple black frames, significant enough for visitors to view. The floors were old pine boards, worn smooth with years of traffic through the door. The window facing the street had 'Green Meadow Times' painted in bold red letters, outlined in black. An orange and yellow striped cat sat in the sun in one corner of the window, atop a stack of papers.

"Can I help you?" An older woman, shuffling her feet as she walked, came toward the front of the building wearing an apron smudged with ink. She wore soft-soled oxfords and dark socks, with her blue printed dress visible beneath the apron. She had gray hair, and her apron emphasized her large torso. As she peered over her glasses at the intruders, Jeff and Carol sensed that they had interrupted her work.

Jeff responded, "My name is Jeff Lipton. I was wondering if you could do some research for me, or if I could do the research myself. I'm trying to find out some information on the Don Ribold family, who used to live here in Green Meadow. We're working on my family ancestry and think the Ribold family is related to us." That seemed like a good line that didn't raise a lot of questions. And to some extent it was the truth, just not the whole story.

"Well, how much information do you have? I can't do research without some dates or some leads on these folks. I remember the name, but didn't know the family personally." The woman put one hand on her hip and the other on her chin, waiting for Jeff to give her some additional data.

Jeff tried to add some charm, and to show this woman how desperate he was. "I'm afraid I only have the year 1975, when Annie Ribold Moss died, and then some time in the years following when the family moved out of town. I thought there might have been something reported in the papers to tell me where they had gone from this area." Jeff's eyes pleaded with her for some help.

"I'll tell you what. I'll show you where all the microfiche is located. It's organized by dates. I don't have time to do the research through all those files, so if you promise to put everything back exactly where you found it, you can go into the library files in the back and do the research yourself. But you have to be careful with those files." She shook her finger at Jeff, emphasizing her concerns, then turned and started toward the back of the building.

Jeff and Carol followed her close behind. "Yes ma'am, I'll be very careful."

Jeff and Carol each sat at a fiche reader, taking separate months starting with 1974. The plan was to look for any reference to the Ribold name. Jeff came across Annie's obituary, which he had already found, from May of 1974. Carol found an ad for the local insurance company, mentioning that Jack Thomas would be assuming most of the accounts serviced by Don Ribold, as Don was going to be moving to Chatsworth to take a position with an insurance company there. The date on the newspaper was September 15, 1975, just a couple of months after Annie's death. They continued to comb through the microfiche, but found no other mention of the Ribolds, and there were other stops they still wanted to make this morning. After putting all the film back in place, Jeff looked for the owner.

"Thanks so much for allowing us to do the research. Is there any possibility that you might have a record of the address for the Ribolds when they moved out of town? Any forwarding address?" Jeff thought there might be a chance.

"They don't subscribe to the paper, and as far as I know, we never had a forwarding address. Sorry." She didn't look up from her work. *Well, probably not that sorry*, Jeff thought. They wove their way back to the front door, wondering why the fire marshal wouldn't have condemned this place.

"So much for that resource," Carol said, as they settled back into the bucket seats of her car. "Let's try the post office."

The post office wasn't much more help than was the newspaper office. The time had been too long for them to have any record on file, if there had been a forwarding address at one time. The next stop was the city hall, if for no other reason than to see if anyone could remember the Ribolds and knew them well enough to know where they had gone. Jeff was getting discouraged.

"Good morning. My name is Jeff Lipton, and I'm looking for some information on a family that used to live here in Green Meadow. I wondered if you might be able to help me." Jeff reached out to shake hands with the lady behind the counter. He didn't hold out much hope that she would give him any additional information.

"Well, Jeff, I've worked in this office for 35 years, so I know just about everyone in this town. My name's Sally Coates. What can I help you with?" Sally had her gray hair pulled back in a tight bun on the back of her neck, with a couple of unruly wisps curled down in front of her ears. She tucked these behind her ears as she stood up from her stool to talk to Jeff.

Jeff noticed that for an older gal, Sally appeared to be in great shape. She was slender, neatly dressed in a fashionable pair of slacks and blouse and wore pierced earrings. She had on little if any makeup, but boasted a good tan and rosy cheeks. She peered at Jeff over her half glasses.

Jeff responded, "I'm looking for the Don Ribold family, who lived here in the 60s and 70s, and moved away in 1974, after the death of their daughter, Annie. We think there is a family tie with the Ribolds, and I'm doing some research." Jeff had the response memorized by this time.

"Sure, I remember the Ribolds," Sally said. "Don worked down here at the insurance office for several years, and I used to see him at Rotary and other events in the city. I didn't know his wife very well. Annie was a beautiful girl. She ran around with Carrie Bloom, and they were college roommates. Carrie married some guy in Minnesota, and I think that's where they live. They were a pair, those two. Don told me once that Annie had run off with some older guy, just about a year after she left for college. They weren't in touch with her at all. Then about six years later, they got word that she was in a hospital and was asking for them, and she died soon after that. The whole thing was really hard on Don and his wife. I never knew the whole story, but Don and Arlene moved out of town to Chatsworth soon after Annie died. There was a lot of speculation, but they kept everything to themselves."

"Would you have any idea of the address of the Ribolds in Chatsworth?" Jeff asked.

"Honey, I sure don't. But I'd bet that if you want to find them, you can find them in a phone book or a city office in Chatsworth. It's a good hour and a half drive from here, though." Sally could see that Jeff was disappointed with what he had heard. She turned to see Tom Vance, the local police chief enter the room. "Tom, this young fellow is looking for the Don Ribold family. Do you remember them, or do you know if they are still in Chatsworth?"

Tom Vance walked toward the counter. He was dressed in his uniform, as he was taking the late Saturday afternoon and evening shift in the patrol car. His hair was white and bushy, and he hiked up his belt as he looked at Jeff and Carol. "Don and Arlene Ribold were good folks. I haven't heard anything about them since they left the area. Are you kin to them?"

"That's what I'm trying to find out," said Jeff. "Do you know what happened to their son, I think his name was Marty?" Sally hadn't mentioned Marty at all.

"Marty left here and went to college after high school. He came back for the first summer to work for Jim at the grocery store, but after that, I never saw anything of him. I remember reading in the paper where he had graduated from college, but I have no idea where he went from there. Annie was a wild one, but Marty was a good kid all through high school. We never had any trouble out of him. Annie made some bad choices for friends." Tom was remembering events of the time, but he thought he had said enough. "I suppose you would have to locate the parents to find out about Marty."

"Thanks for your help," said Jeff, as he shook Tom's hand. He felt his headache returning, as he turned to go out the door. "Come on, Carol, let's go get a Coke."

Carol followed him out the door, and into the car. "You must be feeling very frustrated by now. I'm up for a drive to Chatsworth, if you want to go. But we'll have to get your car. I don't trust my car on the open road. It's got a knock in the engine, and I haven't had it in the shop to find out what it is. Maybe I'm afraid to find out. We could grab a Coke at that Quick Mart. What do you say?"

Jeff looked at Carol. She had been so willing to help him. Why would she care? "Don't you have something better to do today than run around on a wild goose chase with me? You don't have to do this, Carol." He was serious.

"Don't be a dork. Unless you tell me that you don't want me to go along, I'm going. It's like trying to solve a big mystery. And if it will bring you some peace of mind, I'll be happy. What do you say?" Carol looked into Jeff's eyes. She reached out and touched his hand and patted it reassuringly. Her bright blue eyes danced with excitement, and Jeff felt encouraged.

"Then we'll go. Let's take your car to my motel, and we'll take mine. It might get late before we get back. Will it be okay if we leave your car there? I'll mention it to Al at the front desk, so he'll know it's your car. I'm sure it won't be a problem with him."

Carol shifted the car into gear and backed out of the parking space and into the street. They were back at the motel in a few minutes, changed cars, and checked in with Al. They filled up the car at Quick Mart, grabbed two Cokes from the dispenser, and started out in the direction of Chatsworth.

Chapter 5
JEFF IN CHATSWORTH

By the time Jeff and Carol got on the road and then traveled the distance to Chatsworth, about 90 miles, it was mid afternoon. They had talked along the way about any number of things, but little about Annie. Each of them was anxious to learn more about the other. Jeff laughed as he told Carol about his high school days, his adventures at State, and his job.

He told her he had been a good student. He was active in basketball and track, the only two competitive sports offered in his small school, just a short distance away in Aubrey. George Lipton came to every game, and Sue helped with all the team support events, both of them very involved in his life and activities. Their country home had a basketball hoop fastened above the garage door. George played H-O-R-S-E with Jeff some evenings and Sunday afternoons, helping him to gain his skills in defense and offense on the court.

Sue spoiled him with wonderful home-cooked foods, including desserts that always had her guests raving. He never doubted the depth of love they held for him.

Carol talked about high school in Green Meadow and her mother. Her father had abandoned them when she was very young, so she had a good deal of sympathy for Jeff's interest in finding his mother and her family. She had always lived at home and driven to campus for classes. In fact the first years, she had attended the community college, taking a minor load of course, to save on the expense of her education. Her credits all transferred into her junior year, but she had decided to take off the fall semester to build up some money before starting her last two semesters.

Jeff wondered if Carol was dating anyone. She had seemed anxious to help him, and didn't indicate she had a commitment. He wasn't sure how to pose the question to her. Maybe it was best to ask it straight out? "Are you seeing anyone?" Seemed like a simple enough question, but Jeff wasn't sure it was the right time yet. He delighted in her spontaneity and her enthusiasm, as she answered, "No way!"

Carol continued to ramble on about some funny events from her senior trip in high school, until Jeff asked, "Have you ever sung with a band?" Well, it would tell him more about Carol.

"Where did *that* come from?" Carol responded. "How did we get from my high school senior trip to whether I sing with a band?"

"Just a question," Jeff replied.

"Well, actually, I do sing a bit. I have sung with the church choir for some time, and I was with a little band for a while that performed in small towns around here. We had a drummer and two guitarists and me. We haven't been invited to the State Fair as yet, nor do we have a record in the works." She laughed at her own joke. Carol tossed back her blond hair.

They were silent for the last few miles before reaching the edge of Chatsworth. The sun had been shining all afternoon, the rain having moved on to the east. Jeff thought about what he had discovered so far about his mother. Those who knew about Annie as a teenager surely didn't have much good to say. He turned his attention to Carol.

"We're almost there! Let's stop at the first service station we come to, and I'll see if there is anything listed in the phone book. If we can get an address, maybe someone can give us some directions." Jeff wondered if they would find Don Ribold that easily, or if they would be on another tangent before the day was through.

"There's an Amoco station ahead on the right, and it looks like it has some trucker services. That usually means good food and cold drinks, and hopefully a bathroom!" Carol crossed her arms in front of her to indicate the urgency.

Jeff pulled into the service station, driving through to the phone booth on the left of the building. Carol jumped out of the car and ran into the station, calling back, "Can I get you a Coke?"

"Sure. I'll see what I can find out here." Jeff found a small tablet in his glove compartment and went to the phone booth. The phone book was dangled from the sturdy chain in one corner of the booth. Jeff flipped to the "R's" and ran his finger down the listings to find Ribold. And there it was. *Ribold, Don. 2618 Chadron Lane. 825-1649.* He couldn't believe it. Was this the right Don Ribold? Should he call first, or should he see if he could find the address? He decided he should call first. He would just tell the person who answered the phone that he was looking to find a family tie to the Ribold family, and ask if he could stop by. He found some coins, dropped them into the slots and dialed the number.

The phone rang several times. "The party you are trying to reach 'Don Ribold' is not available. Please leave your name and number at the tone."

Jeff panicked and didn't know what to do. He couldn't leave a message, as he wasn't sure this was even the right person, so he hung up the phone. Now what? He turned and went into the service station building, carrying his piece of paper with the address and phone number. Carol was checking out with two Cokes.

"How'd you do?" she asked, taking some money from her purse to pay the cashier for the Cokes.

"I found an address and a phone number, but when I called, I got a recording. I hung up, because I didn't want to leave a message. Shit!" Jeff was frustrated with the outcome, and what to do next.

"Here, give me that piece of paper." Carol took the paper and turned to the cashier. "Can you tell me where this address is here in town?" she asked.

The frumpy cashier looked at Carol, then at the paper she had handed her. "I'm sorry, I don't know the city very well, so am not familiar with Chadron Lane." She gave Carol an apologetic look, handed the paper back to her, and turned to help the next customer.

"Just wanted to pay for some gas," the customer responded. "Ma'am, can I help you with that address?" He turned to Carol, as he reached for his wallet to pay for his gas. He peeled off the money needed for the gas purchase, and walked toward Carol and Jeff.

"I've lived around here for many years, so I know the city pretty well, except for maybe those new subdivisions on the north side. Name's Harlan Little." Harlan shook Carol's hand, then Jeff's.

Carol handed him the address written on the piece of paper. "Chadron, Chadron..... oh, I know where that is. It's on the east side of town, near the high school."

Harlan flipped the paper over and drew a mini map for them, showing the major turns and streets they would find before they reached Chadron. He talked them through the directions as he wrote them out. His hands shook slightly as he wrote, and Carol sensed that he was not in the best of health. His thinning gray hair curled up from beneath the brim of his baseball cap, and his sweatshirt sleeves were worn. She glanced up to look out the window at the cars at the gas pumps, and noted that Harlan's must be the older model Pontiac with the dulled paint and rusted bumper.

"Thanks so much, Harlan," said Jeff. "Can we get you something, like a cup of coffee or a cold drink?"

"A cup of coffee would be nice," Harlan replied. His smile revealed aging teeth, stained with the tobacco he was chewing. Carol walked quickly over to the coffee dispenser, retrieved a cup of coffee for Harlan, and brought it back to the cashier to pay. She then handed the cup to Harlan.

"Thanks again!" Harlan took the coffee, and nodded to Jeff and Carol. He then went out the door and got into his car and drove away. Jeff and Carol watched him go.

Jeff looked down at the paper, then at Carol. "Well, let's take this and see what we can find out." He took her arm and escorted her through the door and out to the car. They followed Harlan's directions carefully, almost missing the turn on Chadron. Harlan wasn't sure which way on Chadron they would go to find 2618, and they quickly realized they had turned the wrong direction. Jeff pulled into a driveway and turned back to go the other direction. The house at 2618 Chadron was a tan brick ranch with the lawn neatly mowed. The porch and the window frames were painted white, and each window was covered with a blind. There were green shutters on the windows. Some tall trees graced the front yard, indicating that the house had been built some time ago. A few marigolds were still blooming, and a trio of pumpkins was nestled in one corner of the porch with some corn stalks. A scarecrow decoration hung on the front door. Jeff parked his car at the end of the sidewalk.

"Looks like a nice place," said Carol, unsure what to say to Jeff at this point.

"Yeah, why don't you stay here, and I'll see if anyone is home. They may not be, since the recorder picked up when I called."

Jeff walked to the front porch and rang the doorbell. He waited, listening. Then he rang the doorbell again. Still no answer.

"Are you looking for the Ribold's?" a voice asked.

Jeff nearly jumped out of his skin. He turned to his right to see a lady dressed in a housecoat and slippers standing on her front porch at the house next door. She was obviously watching over the house for the Ribolds.

"I'm looking for Don Ribold. Is this the right house?" Jeff stepped down from the porch and walked toward the neighbor. He noted that she backed away as he approached, walking toward her front door.

"Don Ribold lives there, but they aren't home. Went up to Des Moines last night, and won't be back until sometime tomorrow." By this time, her hand was on the door knob of her home.

"Thanks, I can come back later," Jeff replied. He didn't walk any closer to her porch.

"Can I tell them you were here?" she asked Jeff.

"No, that's okay. Don doesn't know me. I just found his address and phone number in the phone book, and a nice gentleman at the gas station helped me with directions. I'm from out of town. But thanks, anyway." Jeff waved to her, and walked back to the car. She watched him as he got into the car, and then pulled away.

"Geez, she scared the crap out of me!" Jeff said to Carol, as he got into the car. "Did you see her coming out of the house?"

"I did, but I didn't have time to warn you," Carol laughed. "Looks like the Ribold's have a good watchdog looking after their home while they are gone. Did I hear her say they would be out of town until tomorrow?"

"Yes, that's right. I don't think there's much we can do anymore today. But I'm starved. How about if we find a place where we can get a good meal and a couple of beers before we head back for Green Meadow?" Jeff remembered that they hadn't eaten a good meal since earlier this morning, and he wanted to treat Carol to something nice. "Hungry for anything special?"

"Not really, but a steak would be great!" Carol grinned at him. "I saw a steakhouse on our way here. If we go back on the route we came on, we should be able to find it. I think it was on my side of the street coming here."

Jeff drove back on the route Harlan had provided, and they found the Dixie Steakhouse on Elm Street. Jeff parked the car, and they went into the building. It was a little after 6 PM, and the Saturday night crowd had started to gather. They put in Jeff's name for a table for two in non-smoking, and took two stools at the bar. Jeff ordered a pitcher of beer and two glasses. He wanted to just think about Carol tonight. He was intrigued by her. She seemed to be so self-assured and independent. Yet she was working in a diner for low wages and tips. She couldn't be saving all that much money for college working there. And those beautiful blue eyes. Her blond hair was long and silky. She could leave it down or pull it back, and she was beautiful either way. Jeff felt a longing for her, as he watched her slip onto the bar stool and dangle her feet. Her jeans were tight and her v-neck sweater revealed the cleavage between her breasts. He watched her as she took a sip of the beer.

"Mmmmm, that tastes good. It feels good to just sit and relax, doesn't it?" She looked at Jeff and caught his glance. She could understand Jeff's frustration with finding family. Carol had not seen her father since she was a small child. His parents came to see her once in a while, and sometimes she had gone to see them in the summer, but not since she was a teenager. Yet Jeff had a family, an adoptive family. Carol wondered how his adoptive mother felt about his search for his real mother. Jeff was incredibly handsome, with his dark curls. She was glad he didn't cut them all off like so many guys. Carol was attracted to him.

They sipped the beer and talked for 20 minutes or so before their dinner was ready. At the table, Jeff ordered a bottle of red wine to accompany their steak dinner. They talked and laughed as they downed the beer, the wine, and the steak dinner, suddenly realizing how long they had been in the restaurant. Yet they stopped in the bar for one more round of beer before deciding to leave. The evening had been a welcome relief from the last two days for Jeff.

"We can't drive back to Green Meadow anymore tonight. I've had a little too much to drink, and I'm pretty tired." Jeff looked at Carol for a solution.

"I saw a motel on the edge of town as we came in," she said. "We can get a room there and decide what you want to do tomorrow morning. The room is so that we can s-l-e-e-p, mind you." Carol smiled at Jeff. *We'll see,* he thought to himself. There was something about Carol that kept him from pushing her into intimacy too soon.

Carol drove Jeff's car back to the motel on the highway, and pulled into the parking lot. "Will you be okay to get the room?" she asked him.

"I think so. I'll be right back." Jeff checked to see that his wallet was in his pocket, and went into the motel entrance while Carol waited in the car. He returned within a few minutes with a key and some papers in his hand. "I've got the key to the room, along with a map of the city for reference. Would you drive around to the second entrance, so we don't have far to walk?" Jeff pointed out the direction for Carol to drive. "I got a room with two beds, so we can s-l-e-e-p!" Jeff teased her.

They drove around to the second entrance, locked up the car, and found the room. Jeff turned the entry key in the room lock, and opened the door for Carol. "After you, ma'am," he said, stumbling slightly as he followed her into the room.

"I get the one closest to the window," said Carol, going into the bathroom and closing the door behind her. Jeff could hear her running water into the sink and washing her face. In a few minutes she came out, wiping her face dry with a hand towel. Jeff had never seen anyone so beautiful. Wisps of blonde hair were dampened and clung to her face. She certainly did not need makeup for those blue eyes. Jeff reached for her hand.

"Carol, you are beautiful, and I can't tell you how much I appreciate you coming here with me. I'm not sure I could have done it without you; I would probably still be stuck in Green Meadow wondering what to do next. Would you mind terribly if I kissed you?" Jeff pulled her toward him. He didn't wait for her response, but lifted her chin to kiss her. She did not pull away, but responded to his kiss.

Jeff put his arms around her and pulled her to him, kissing her more deeply, and opening her mouth with his. She pulled away from him, taking both of his hands in hers. "S-l-e-e-p, remember?" she asked. She walked away from him, slipped out of her sweater and slacks, crawled under the covers, and said, "Good-night, Jeff."

"Good-night," Jeff responded, unable to believe that this beautiful woman had just stripped down to her panties and bra and climbed into a bed next to his and was going to sleep. And he was going to let her!

Chapter 6
SUMMER OF 1969

Don Ribold had gone to the police to see if they could help he and Arlene find Annie. The police had told him there was little they could do. Annie was of age, and lots of kids were running away from home to get away from their parents and small town living. They assured Don that Annie would be in touch and would probably be back. Arlene was furious at herself for giving Annie an ultimatum, and was sick with worry about her well-being. She prayed that Annie would contact them to let them know she was okay. But they heard nothing.

Annie and Mark moved into a tiny apartment on the second floor in a small town in New York. Mark got a job at the local Readi-Warehouse store, and Annie set up housekeeping. Annie knew that Mark didn't make a lot at Readi-Warehouse, but he seemed to always have a lot of money in his pocket. Finally, one day she had the nerve to ask him about it.

"Mark, where does all that other money come from? Are you selling drugs?" Annie wasn't sure if Mark would tell her the truth. He sat down beside her on the couch.

"Annie, just know I love you. I've got some guys I'm doing some work for. They bring things to me at the warehouse, and I pack them up and deliver for them. I don't ask any questions, and they give me money under the table. And we can get all the drugs we want as well. It's pretty safe, as it's not enough stuff to bring up any questions. These paid for most of my way through school." Mark had been matter-of-fact about it. "All the better to take care of you, my beauty!" he had replied, and kissed her.

"But don't you want to get a job in engineering?" Annie had asked him.

"Sure, but I have plenty of time to do that. I'm working in the contractor supplies area, so maybe that will lead to something someday. Right now, we have plans to make for Woodstock next month. Remember I told you about the big music show – 'Three Days of Peace and Music'?" Mark was excited about the event.

On August 14th, Mark packed up the trunk of the car and the back seat with their bags, a small tent, and some sleeping bags. Annie packed a cooler with beer, cheese, ham, and some fruit and they headed out for Bethel. There were so many cars that Mark had to park a long distance back on Route 17B, make several trips with all their belongings, and set up the tent with Annie's help. The music started around 5 PM on the 15th, and Mark and Annie were caught up in the fray of thousands of young people, drinking beer, smoking pot, and making love. They snuggled up in the small tent as the rains came down on Friday night, but woke up for more music and partying on Saturday.

When the rain started again on Sunday, they returned to their car. Mark decided to leave the sleeping bags and the tent behind, and just grabbed the cooler and what was left of his supplies. Mark showed Annie the wad of money he had collected with the drugs. "Look at this, honey. There's more money there than most people handle in a year."

"What are you going to do with all that money?" Annie asked.

"Most of it goes to my supplier. They knew we would have a lot of buyers this weekend, so they advanced me some stuff. Someone will be by the warehouse to pick it up on Monday." Mark acted as though the transactions were a normal business.

"Mark, it makes me nervous to see you involved with this. Aren't you concerned about getting caught? Some of those guys are kind of ruthless."

"As long as I pay up and no one knows the source, I won't have any problems." Mark got back onto the highway to drive back to their apartment. They were both exhausted from the weekend's events. Annie laid her head on his shoulder and fell asleep.

On Monday, Annie decided she would look for a job. Mark was gone so much, and she needed something to do. She had picked up a copy of the New York Times Sunday paper and the local Classifieds, and had circled a couple of ads where she thought she might be able to get hired. Several were within walking distance of the apartment. She stopped by the bookstore, the bank, the insurance office, and the library, and filled out an application at each of them. At both the bookstore and the insurance office, she was able to talk to the owners, and she really liked the owner of the bookstore. The hours were good, and the pay was decent for a job so close to home. She stopped by the deli a block from the apartment and ordered an iced tea with lemon, no sugar.

"Don't you live in the Oaks apartment building on Second Street?" a young woman spoke to Annie.

"Yes, I do. Have we met there?" Annie was trying to remember where she had seen her before. Annie noticed that she wore her long, brown hair in pigtails, and had a beret on her head. It seemed to Annie that it was a bit warm for the hat. She was attractive, in a simple sort of way, and wore almost no makeup.

Her brown eyes were round and expressive, her faced tanned from the summer sun. She wore a short skirt and simple over blouse with some platform shoes.

"I've seen you in the laundry room before, and maybe in the halls. I'm Laurie Cameron. I live in 2G." Laurie extended her right hand to Annie.

Taking her hand, Annie said, "I'm in 2B, just down the hall. I'm Annie Ribold. I knew I had seen you somewhere before, but was having trouble placing you. My boyfriend and I were at that big Woodstock show this weekend, so I'm still a little out of it. Do you live alone?"

"Yes. I'm divorced and have two cats in the apartment with me. I work at the bank on 10th Avenue in the trust department. I'm just taking a quick coffee break, and then have to get back to work." Laurie smiled at Annie, showing her perfect teeth. "Why don't you just come on over and knock on my door sometime, and we'll get together?"

"Okay, sure. My boyfriend works a lot of hours at Readi-Warehouse, so I'd love the company. I'll see how things go today, and maybe I'll stop by this evening. I was at your bank today to put in an application, but I haven't had an interview as yet. I need to get a job to keep myself busy." *It wouldn't hurt if Laurie could help her out*, Annie thought.

"I'll see if there is anything I can do for you. I've been there for five years now, but that job's in a different department. Hope I see you later on this evening." Laurie picked up her coffee from the counter, and waved as she went out the front door.

Laurie was the first female acquaintance for Annie since she and Mark had arrived in Wahlberg. She had stayed in the apartment most of the time, waiting for Mark to get home, and then spending her time with him. The idea of having someone else to talk to excited Annie. She hadn't had any contact with her parents, and she had not called Carrie either. She didn't want to call her friend while she was at home during the summer, but would instead wait until she returned to college in the fall, so that no one would know she was contacting her.

Annie thought briefly about her family. Her mother had made her so angry, and she could still hear herself yelling at her before hanging up the phone when she had called to tell them she was leaving with Mark. She was pleased with the fact that she had stood up to her. There was no way she was going to need her parents again. Marty would be going into his senior year of high school. He was probably still completely clean and following all the rules, always pleasing his parents. She wondered if she could contact him some day. Carrie would have the scoop on everything that was happening in Green Meadow when she talked to her next month.

Annie finished her iced tea and headed back to the apartment building. She gathered up a few clothes and carted them down to the laundry room, grabbing a magazine to read while the clothes were washing. She decided to sit in the laundry room and move the clothes from the washer to the dryer, then fold them, before returning to the apartment. Annie watched an ant crawl across the floor and under the dryer, where lint had gathered from so many washings. Something sticky had been spilled on the floor, and had also collected a dusting of lint. The block walls were painted sunshine yellow, with graffiti and stenciling for added interest. The chairs were turquoise bucket seats with chrome legs, the laundry carts wire mesh with casters. A table among the chairs held a variety of magazines, some from several months before. The floor was concrete, painted a rusty brown. The dryer buzzer sounded to alert Annie to remove the clothes. She folded them, placed them in her laundry basket, and climbed the two flights of stairs to the apartment 2B.

Inside the apartment, Annie could smell the stew cooking in the crock pot. She was trying to learn some cooking skills to fix Mark some decent meals. The crock pot was her best friend at the moment in the kitchen. A recipe book came with it from the store, and she was able to get the supplies and understand the instructions to make some pretty tasty food. Annie thought perhaps Laurie might be able to help her out in that department, since she was a little older than Annie, and probably more experienced in cooking.

Mark came home around 5:30, picked her up and swung her around. "Things are good, baby!" he exclaimed. "You are beautiful and sexy, and you can cook, too! I've died and gone to heaven!" Mark kissed her and caressed her butt, drawing her to him. He could feel his excitement growing, as she returned his kiss and pressed herself against him. He picked her up and carried her to the bedroom, unzipped her skirt, and slid his hand inside her panties.

"I've missed you," Annie said. She unbuttoned her blouse and unhooked her bra. She reached for Mark's belt buckle, and then his zipper to release him.

Mark stripped off his T-Shirt, slid out of his pants, and stood before Annie, seated on the edge of the bed. She giggled, and flopped back onto the bed. Mark knelt between her thighs and kissed her breasts and her tummy. Then he pulled himself forward, entering her with enough force to make Annie cry out with pleasure.

After their love making, Annie told him she had dinner ready for him. It was a new recipe she had found in the crock cookbook. She was also anxious to tell Mark about Laurie, who had introduced herself to her today.

"I wondered why you had a bra on," Mark teased, after Annie told him she had been out job hunting earlier. "I have to go back to work for a while, but I'll be back in about two hours. Why don't you go down the hall and get acquainted with Laurie. I'd like to see you make some new friends here."

Annie decided it would be a great idea, and she was anxious to get to know Laurie a little better. She would be guarded about her own family situation, not knowing yet whether her parents were trying to locate her. They finished their dinner, and Mark headed out the door to return to the warehouse.

Annie knocked on the door of 2G. "Anyone home?" she asked. The hall outside the apartment was dark and uninviting, with paneling on the bottom half of the walls and dark, flocked wallpaper on the top half. A light fixture held a naked bulb above the name plate by the door to 2G. It read 'Cameron'. The carpet on the floor was a runner, leaving bare wood on the sides. It was worn and dirty, stained with any variety of liquid spills. Annie heard footsteps approaching the door.

"Who is it?" came the voice from inside, Laurie's voice.

"It's Annie Ribold. We met today at the deli." Annie was a little nervous about this meeting. She wasn't sure why. Maybe it was just anticipation.

The door lock clicked and Annie could hear the chain lock rattling. "Great, Annie. Come on in!" Laurie seemed glad to see her.

The apartment had an instant charm about it. Laurie obviously had some experience in decorating. Although not the newest in furniture, it was neatly arranged, and had lamps and pillows and throws in all the right places. A lava lamp bubbled on one end table, with large blue bubbles floating in yellowish oil. Annie could smell the distinct aroma of incense burning somewhere in the room. There was a variety of posters hanging on the walls. One in particular caught Annie's eye. It was a silhouette of a woman in black and white with a red hat and gloves. Another was a poster from "Tommy". The windows in the room were very tall, as in Annie's apartment, but Laurie had the windows draped with a sheer curtain, tied back near the sill, and billowing lazily with the breeze from the open window. A large orange and yellow cat sprawled on the end of the sofa. Laurie even had a flower arrangement sitting in the middle of her kitchen table, along with a napkin holder and some glass salt and pepper shakers.

"Come join me, while I finish my dinner." Laurie called back over her shoulder as she walked ahead of Annie into the kitchen. She motioned for Annie to have a seat. "What can I get you to drink, a beer?" She walked to the refrigerator and stood with it open, waiting for Annie's response.

"Sure, that would be great. Your apartment is rad!" Annie kept glancing around the rooms of the apartment in admiration. The kitchen was tiny but adequate, just a little smaller than Annie's. There were canisters for the usual flour and sugar, a cookie jar shaped like a bee hive, and a crock with various kitchen utensils sticking out of it. Annie wondered if Laurie was a good cook. "Have you lived here long? The apartment looks like you have been here for some time."

"I've been here ever since my divorce was final. We used to live on the other side of town. I brought one of my cats with me, and found the other one about a year ago, wandering behind the apartment building. Muffin likes to hide when I have company, so you may not see her at all while you are here. Sugar is the one on the couch. She's about 8 years old now." Laurie handed Annie a beer from the refrigerator and sat down to finish her meal. She had warmed up some leftover meatloaf and fixed a quick lettuce salad. "How old are you, Annie?" she asked.

"I'm 19 and a half. I met Mark last year in school. He was a senior, and I was just a freshman at Iowa State. We came out here after his graduation." Annie was weighing her words, unsure of how much to share with Laurie at this point.

"He's a good looking guy, that's for sure. I've seen him coming and going from the building. You said he is just your boyfriend, though. Do your parents know you are living together?" Laurie was inquisitive.

"I haven't seen my parents since Easter weekend. We had sort of a falling out, and I haven't been home or been in touch with them. There is no way they would have allowed me to go away with Mark, that's for sure. But we are doing okay. I don't need them."

"Hmmm. That's pretty rough, Annie. My parents live in New York City. I don't see too much of them, but we are on pretty decent terms. My dad's an attorney, and Mom's a socialite, spending all her time with the hoity-toity ladies of New York. I left home at 18 to go to college, and never went back much after that. I met my ex in college, and we got married way too young. We had this big wedding with all the trimmings. It only lasted for about a year. We were both trying to go to school, and we weren't meant to be married. No kids. It was a good time to break it off. I got this job at the bank soon after that, and they helped me finish school here in Wahlberg. I don't make a lot of money, but I've gotten some promotions along the way, and didn't even have to screw the bosses to get them! The trust department is kind of interesting. We handle money for all the rich bitches here in the city." Laurie paused to take a couple of bites of her dinner. "What does Mark do?"

"He works at Readi-Warehouse," Annie said. "He has a degree in engineering, but he hasn't found anything yet in that field. He works some odd hours and has to be gone a lot in the evening."

"I can't believe you two went to Woodstock! I know there were tons of people going. Some of my friends from down at the bar were heading up there, but I haven't seen them since they got back. Tell me all about it." Laurie leaned forward into her dinner, ready to listen as Annie told her about the weekend. Annie was excited to tell her about the music and the crowds, and the rains that nearly drowned them all, as well as the open use of drugs. While Annie was talking, Laurie finished her meal and took her dishes over to the sink and washed them. She came back to the table, toting another beer for Annie, and a fresh one for herself. Laurie lit up a cigarette.

"Oh, I almost forget to tell you!" Laurie stopped Annie. "I talked to the personnel gal today at the bank, and told her all about you, at least what I knew about you, which was very little. In any case, she told me she would call you for an interview. How about that?" Laurie was excited for Annie and pleased that she could have some influence.

"No kidding? That would be great! I need something to do, and I'd like to have some of my own money, you know? Mark's okay with me getting a job. Maybe I'll go back to school sometime like you did. Thanks so much, Laurie." Annie reached out and touched Laurie's arm.

Laurie placed her hand over Annie's. "No problem. Glad to help out. We have to get together often. I've got some weed. Want to share a joint?"

Annie felt very relaxed, but glanced at the clock. It was 7:30, and still very bright outside. "Okay," she said, following Laurie into the living room. Laurie put a Bob Dylan album on the stereo, opened a box on a shelf and took out a cigarette wrapper and a small bag of marijuana. She wrapped the joint and lit it, inhaling deeply. Then she handed it to Annie, and they passed it between them as they listened to the music. Laurie reached out and held Annie's hand. They were startled to hear a knock on the door.

Laurie made sure the joint was snuffed out, and got up to go to the door. "Who's there?" she asked, leaning her ear to the door.

"It's Mark Moss from 12B. Is Annie in there with you?" Mark waited for the apartment door to open.

"Yup, Annie's here." Laurie opened the door and stepped aside to let Mark in. Annie stood up from the couch and walked toward him.

"Laurie and I have been having a great visit, Mark. I'm sure we will all be good friends." Annie was happy to see Mark, but a little disappointed that her time with Laurie was ending.

"Got time for a beer, Mark?" Laurie asked.

"Another time, maybe, thanks. I'm beat and want to get a shower and hit the sack. Thanks for watching over Annie for me," he said, as he took Annie's arm to walk her out the door.

"Laurie, I'll see you later. And I'll let you know if I hear from the bank. Thanks for everything!" Annie was cheerful as she and Mark walked back to their apartment. While Mark was in the shower, Annie thought back over the evening and her time in Laurie's apartment. She was really a neat gal, and Annie looked forward to spending more time with her.

The next morning, Annie got a call to go to the bank for an interview with personnel, got herself dressed in her most conservative outfit, and walked the short distance to the bank on Thursday. She felt the interview went pretty well. The personnel lady, Sue Ellen Gifford, walked Annie back to the main door of the bank, so she didn't get a chance to see Laurie. Mark was home that evening, so she felt she had so much to share with him. On Friday, the phone rang, and Sue Ellen offered Annie the job in the bank operations area, working with the check processing. Annie was elated. She nearly knocked Mark over when he came in the door, wrapping her arms around his neck and her legs around his waist.

"I got a job today at the bank and I start on Monday. Now you have to take me out to dinner!" Annie exclaimed.

They walked the few blocks to the bar that Laurie had told Annie about. The Blue Goose was buzzing with people. Mark and Annie ordered a fish dinner with fries and onion rings, along with a beer. Laurie and some of her friends joined them. Laurie was watching Mark and noted that he had gone to the men's room with one of the guys at the table, who was getting into stronger drugs. Laurie suspected that Mark was dealing, and had supplied the goods.

The TV in the bar was still relating the events of August: Charles Manson and his "Helter Skelter", Hurricane Camille in Mississippi, and an oil spill off Santa Barbara, California. The air was thick with smoke and the smell of a variety of liquors. Most of the group at the table was unaffected by the news, beginning to feel the effects of the liquor as they chattered about the war in Vietnam, President Nixon, and the "establishment" in general. Annie was glad to be a part of this group.

Chapter 7
THE RIBOLDS

Jeff awoke to a burst of light streaming in through the now-open drapes. Carol was up and dressed, and had pulled on the rope to open them.

"Wake up, sunshine!" she said, as she threw a pillow at Jeff. Carol had obviously already been into the shower, and Jeff wondered how long she had been up. "I've already had my shower and brushed my teeth with a freebie brush from the motel, so I'm ready to get some breakfast!"

Jeff pulled the pillow over his face. "Let me sleep!" he said. "I had too much to drink last night."

Carol leaned over him with a cup of coffee. "Here's the remedy for that, my dear Jeff. I picked this up at the office just for you. I've already had mine." She handed the coffee to Jeff, who was sitting up by this time on the bed, dressed only in his white briefs, with the coverlet from the bed draped across his lap. His curly dark hair was flattened to his head on one side, and his brown eyes were bloodshot. "You look like hell!"

"Thank you very much. And would you mind looking out the window while I get into the bathroom and freshen up a bit?" Jeff felt an urgency to rush to the bathroom to relieve his screaming bladder. As Carol turned toward the window, he grabbed his jeans from the pile on the floor and hurried into the john.

Carol smiled as she looked out the window at the traffic flowing by the motel. No one would ever believe this. Here she was in the motel with this handsome guy, with no pajamas or clean clothes, and they were behaving as brother and sister. She glanced back to catch a glimpse of Jeff's well-rounded butt and strong legs as he made a dash for the bathroom. She was quite sure she wouldn't let this happen a second time.

Jeff came out of the bathroom shirtless, but at least had put on his jeans. He picked up his shirt from a chair near the dresser, slipped it on, and sat down to put on his socks and shoes. "Did you bring along some aspirin, too?" he asked, grinning at Carol.

"No, but I'm sure some breakfast will help out, along with lots more coffee. I spotted a Waffle House about three blocks down the street, and they should be open for business." She handed him a toiletry bag from her purse. "Here's some deodorant and some mouthwash, and you are welcome to use my hair brush."

"You are a lifesaver!" Jeff exclaimed. He took the bag from Carol and went back into the bathroom to freshen up. Carol watched him as he finished dressing. His muscles rippled as he pulled his shirt together and buttoned it. His hands were strong and he buttoned the shirt quickly. Then he tucked it in his pants, fastened his belt, and was ready to go.

"I'm sure you dressed much faster than I could have." Carol's hair was still damp from the shower, and was pulled back into a pony tail at her neckline. Jeff observed that her skin was radiant, pure peaches and cream complexion. She had a small mole on her left cheekbone. Her eye lashes were long and curled naturally against her eyelids, and she wore a blue eye shadow that enhanced the blue of her eyes. Despite the fact that she had worn the same clothes the day before, she looked unbelievably refreshed.

They drove to the Waffle House where Carol ordered a waffle, while Jeff ordered the omelet special. The waitress brought coffee for them.

"So what's on the agenda for the day?" Carol asked. "The Ribolds aren't due back for a while today, so we probably have some time to kill. Let's ask the waitress what's going on in town."

"Can you tell us if there is anything happening here in Chatsworth today? We are just passing through and have some time to stay around for a while." Carol glanced at Jeff as she asked the waitress for some ideas.

"Down at the park they are having an 'Arts in the Park' event. I think it starts at about 10 and goes to later on this afternoon sometime. There are a bunch of exhibitors set up down there, and there is some music and stuff planned," the waitress explained. "I went last year, and it was pretty good. Other than that, you can take a paddle boat or a row boat out on the lake there at the park, too."

"Well, there you have it. Thanks!" Carol turned to Jeff. "What do you think? We can see the Arts in the Park followed by a romantic paddle boat ride around the lake?" She smiled at Jeff, her eyes alive with excitement. "Then we can get down to the real purpose for our visit to Chatsworth."

Jeff and Carol finished their breakfast. Jeff was a little preoccupied with the prospect of finding his grandparents. He had shown Carol the picture from Annie's things of the older couple, who would now be more than 30 years older than in the picture, making them probably into their late 70s. Would he recognize them if they were, in fact, his grandparents? What would their reaction be to his announcement that he was Florence Ann Ribold Moss' son, *their* grandson. He paid the tab and took Carol's hand as they walked out to the car. It was nearly 10 by this time, so the park should be open for the Art Fair. It would help to pass the time until later this afternoon.

The Art Fair was a mix of oil paintings, photography, jewelry, weaving, and pottery with a smattering of other arts and crafts. Carol picked up a pair of unusual earrings, and Jeff found a black and white photograph of a snow scene that he thought would look nice framed in his office. They rented a paddle boat and laughed as they maneuvered it around the lake. The sun was warm for a late fall day, and the air was crisp and clear. Carol was glad she had brought along a sweater, as the lake breeze was chilly. Jeff wore his leather jacket, and wrapped it around their shoulders as they paddled around the lake. They ate hot dogs and elephant ears for lunch and later shared a bag of popcorn from a vendor. Around 3 in the afternoon, Jeff glanced at his watch and looked around for a phone booth. He spotted one by the pavilion.

"I'm going to try this number to see if the Ribolds are home," he told Carol. "Want to wait here for me?" He took her hand and kissed her lightly on the lips.

"Sure, I'll grab one of these park benches and hold it down until you get back." Carol felt he needed to make the call on his own.

Jeff walked to the pavilion and dropped coins into the slot of the pay phone. Hearing the dial tone, he dialed the number. One ring, two rings, then, "Hello?" the voice on the phone answered. Jeff swallowed hard.

"Hello, my name is Jeff Lipton. Is this Don Ribold?" he asked, a slight tremor in his voice.

"Yes it is. Can I help you?" Don Ribold replied.

"I'm from over in Aubrey and am doing some research on my family history. I wondered if I might stop by to visit briefly with you."

"I don't think I know anyone from Aubrey, Jeff. But I'll be glad to talk to you. Are you in town now?" Don had just gotten home from their weekend trip, and wasn't too anxious for company.

"Yes, I am, if it wouldn't be too much of an inconvenience, I'd like to stop by this afternoon." Jeff was hoping Don would be receptive.

"Well, I'm a little tired, but you can come by. We've been out of town this weekend, doing a lot of driving. Why don't you give me about an hour to rest up a bit, and then you can come over. Do you have my address?"

"Yes, I do. I stopped by last night, but your neighbor told me you were out of town. I have a friend with me, and we'll be by in about an hour. Thanks so much, Mr. Ribold." Jeff heard a click on the other end of the phone line, and hung up the pay phone. The coins clinked into the machine. Jeff walked back across the park lawn to where Carol was waiting for him.

"Did you reach them?" Carol asked.

"Yes, and we can go over there in about an hour. I am really nervous about this. I keep thinking about what

I might have missed by never knowing these people. I have grandparents with my adoptive parents, but I've always felt that the natural grandchildren by my parents' brothers and sisters were their favorites. They were always good to me, but there was something missing, you know?"

"That might be totally your imagination. Let's get something to drink, and I'll help you think through what you will say to the Ribolds when you meet them." Carol once again took charge of the situation.

Jeff and Carol talked over Jeff's approach to the Ribolds, but both of them knew that whatever plans they might lay out, to see the people face to face might blow the plans completely. They did agree that Jeff needed to go slowly, giving them a chance to talk about Annie and the rest of their family. Then Jeff might have an opening in which he could tell them who he was and show them the birth certificate. Perhaps they might even have an idea about the key that was among the things Annie had given the Liptons. At about ten minutes to four, they climbed into the car and drove to the Ribold address.

Carol walked with Jeff to the front porch, and Jeff pressed the doorbell. It was all he could do to keep his voice steady when he saw Don Ribold. Despite the aging, this was the man in the photograph.

"You must be Jeff Lipton? We've been expecting you. I'm Don Ribold." Don extended his hand to Jeff, then to Carol.

"I'm Carol Braun. I live over in Green Meadow, and work there at Peggy's Diner." Carol shook Don's hand, and the two of them followed him into the foyer of the house.

Jeff's eyes quickly took in the living room to the right of the foyer. The room was beautifully decorated in current fashion. Rich leather chairs accented an overstuffed couch. The coffee and end tables were cherry wood. An oil landscape graced the mantel of the fireplace, and a large urn of flowers stood on the right side of the hearth. On the left were the brass tools and a brass ash bucket with ceramic on the handle. The carpeting was neutral and plush. An antique table stood in the bay window facing the street, with a lace cloth runner on the top and a silk floral arrangement in the center. To the left of the foyer was a formal dining room with a matching set of cherry hutch and table with chairs. A huge arrangement of white calla lilies was centered on a table runner that was matched to the chair covers. Crystal and china were carefully placed in the windows of the hutch cupboard. Jeff suspected that there was probably a buffet on the opposite wall. Drapes in both rooms were obviously custom made to accent the colors in the rooms.

"Welcome to our home," said Don Ribold. "If you'll follow me into the family room, you can make yourself comfortable. I'll get my wife."

"Wow! This is quite a place," exclaimed Carol. "The front side looks pretty unassuming, but this is gorgeous inside. And the back yard!" Carol looked around the room to appreciate all the comfortable surroundings. The window facing the back yard was shaded by the roof of the patio, and looked out across the extensive back yard. The landscaping was manicured, with only a small amount of falling leaves dotting the thick carpet of grass. Fall flowers bloomed on the berms surrounding the yard, and a tiny water fall trickled down over some rocks into a small pond in the right corner. Grasses of various colors and density arched over rocks along the sides of the pond and dipped their leaves into the water. Massive trees provided shade for the enormous hostas on the left side of the yard. A stone walkway provided access to the garden and the gazebo, where a porch swing moved in time with the fall breeze. Carol decided she could grab a book and sit there while Jeff visited with these folks. Nice place.

"Jeff and Carol, this is my wife Sophie," said Don Ribold, as he came into the room. The name completely caught Jeff and Carol off guard.

"How do you do, Sophie," said Jeff, trying not to babble like an idiot. Carol knew also that 'Sophie' was not the name they were expecting to hear.

Don motioned for them to sit down. "Now tell me what brings you to Chatsworth." Don sat in a recliner across from Jeff that almost swallowed him in its cushions.

"I, er...." Jeff had a little trouble getting his thoughts together. "My folks and I have been working on some family history, and we came across the Ribold name. I wondered if you could tell me a little about your family: parents and children."

"Well, let's see. My dad's name was John, and his father's name was Joseph Ribold. Joseph came to the U.S. from Germany in the late 1800's. My mother's family was Springer, also German ancestry, from Ostfriesland. They all settled in Iowa as farmers and craftsmen. Somewhere I have some information typed up on my family, as I've done a bit of research on my own. My first wife's family was from England; the James family. Arlene used to say they probably fought the Americans in the Revolutionary War. I'm not sure when her family came to America, but probably a long time before the Ribolds. We had two children. Annie died very young, and our son, Martin, lives in Staley and works in an architectural firm there. Annie is actually buried in Green Meadow where you live, Carol."

Jeff had been taking some notes in a small notebook. "If you could get me a copy of that information, I'd really appreciate it." He looked at Don Ribold. He saw there a reflection of himself in some ways. The dark hair was now very gray, but the physical build and the smile were all the same as in the picture he had of him.

"Sure. You all can get acquainted, while I look for that and make a copy. Sophie can get you something to drink. This might take a few minutes." Don lifted himself out of the recliner and started to walk out of the family room. "Just make yourself at home."

Sophie excused herself to go into the kitchen. Jeff and Carol looked at each other. "He is Annie's father. But what happened to Arlene?" Jeff whispered to Carol, his head swimming. Sophie came into the family room, carrying a tray of iced tea and some glasses, and a plate of cookies. Sophie had graying hair and was impeccably dressed in a skirt and blouse with elegant jewelry. She wore a charm bracelet that had pictures of young children, probably grandchildren. The bracelet jingled as she placed the tray on the coffee table in front of Jeff and Carol.

"Here you are. Tell me more about yourselves. Don tells me you are from Aubrey, Jeff?" Sophie was curious about the pair.

"I am. I work there at a car dealership, and am buying into the business. The owner and I have worked together for some time, and I've been there since I got out of college. Carol is from Green Meadow, and we met just recently." Jeff liked Sophie. She had a lovely smile and a gentle manner that put you immediately at ease with her. "What about you, Sophie? Have you and Don been married a long time?"

"Oh, no. We've only been married a few years. Don's wife, Arlene, died of cancer, and I lost my husband a few years back. We actually knew each other some time ago, but that's a long story. We have so much in common. I'm afraid I don't know much about his family history."

"Well, that's great!" Jeff smiled at her. He stirred some sugar into his iced tea and took a cookie from the plate, handing the plate to Carol. "Are you working outside the home, or are you a homemaker?" Jeff didn't want to offend her by asking if she were retired.

"I work a lot outside the home, but not for money. I have some pet organizations where I volunteer, and it keeps me pretty busy. I do some writing, plus I do all the gardening. Gardening is my joy, and I've been working on this yard for many years. Don moved into this home with me when we got married, and sold his condo. I couldn't part with my garden." Sophie beamed.

"It is absolutely beautiful," Carol told her. "I can't believe you do all this work yourself! I figured you had a full-time gardener."

"Don't I wish! It's almost too much for me, as I find that my knees don't appreciate crawling around among the plants anymore." Sophie laughed at her comment on aging.

"Here we go. I found the pages pretty quickly. A cousin of mine had put this family history together some time ago and gave it to me. So tell me, Jeff, where does your family fit into this picture?" Don handed Jeff the copy and sat back down in the recliner.

Jeff knew he was trapped, and that there was no turning back at this point. "I've been doing some searching, Don, on my own family history. You see, I was adopted by George and Sue Lipton in 1975, when I was just 4 years old. Recently I asked some questions about my real parents, and they gave me a copy of a birth certificate with my mother's name on it. My mother's name was Florence Ann Ribold Moss." Jeff caught Don's eyes as his revelation sunk in.

"What? That's my Annie! It can't be! Let me see that birth certificate." Don sat forward in his chair in amazement. Jeff unfolded a copy of the birth certificate he had been carrying in his pocket and handed it to Don.

"Florence Ann Moss. Right here on the birth certificate. How could Annie have had a child and never told us?" Don looked at Jeff, then at Sophie, for the answer to that question.

"I'm afraid I can't answer that, Don. I have so many questions in my mind as to why she gave me up for adoption, and I was hoping you could help me out with some of those questions. I've had a wonderful life with the Mom and Dad, and they know I am researching my natural family. They have been so good to me. But you understand I need to find more answers about my mother and perhaps my father, and their families." Carol linked her arm through Jeff's for support, but said nothing. Sophie put her hand on Don's shoulder and looked at the document.

"You are my grandson? This is just too unbelievable. Sophie, would you and Carol give Jeff and me some time? Maybe you could rustle up some supper, if they will have time stay here longer?" He looked to Jeff for an answer.

"We can stay. Thanks, Sophie." Jeff watched them walk out into the kitchen and turned back to Don. "I had no idea how I was going to spring all this on you."

"Jeff, I'm 75 years old and retired. I have had so much tragedy in my family. Annie was estranged from us for almost six years. Her mother and I tried to get in touch with her, but she managed to keep us out of her life. There is so much we need to talk about. I'll be glad to help you all I can, but I'm afraid I don't have all the answers. We never even met your father. We just knew that Annie had run away with him and was living somewhere out east. The police told us that since she was over 18, they wouldn't get involved in trying to locate her. We always thought she would come back, but we didn't see her until we got a call late one night from a police officer letting us know that Annie had asked for us. But that's all such a long story. For right now, I want to learn more about you and your adoptive family."

Jeff and Don talked about the present and Jeff's history. Don told Jeff about Arlene's death to uterine cancer, and their fight to keep her alive. They had moved away from Green Meadow after Annie's death to start over. Marty was out on his own, so they thought it would be a good move for them. And they managed pretty well for about ten years until Arlene found out she had cancer. Don had continued in the insurance business, getting into the high risk business arena, and had been very successful. He retired when Arlene became ill, so that he could care for her.

"Would you fellows like to join us for a bite to eat?" Carol had stepped into the room. She noted that Don and Jeff were deep into conversation, and wasn't sure if she should interrupt.

"I'm starved, how about you, Jeff?" Don stood up and motioned to Jeff to follow him into the kitchen. They gathered around the kitchen table, near the patio doors to the back deck, and enjoyed sandwiches and soup that Sophie and Carol had prepared. They chatted like old friends. After supper, Jeff announced that they should be getting back to Green Meadow, so Carol could work on Monday. He told Don that he had taken Monday off as well, but if Don had some plans for the day, he would do some more research on other leads. Perhaps he could meet up with him the next weekend.

They decided that Jeff would drive over to Chatsworth again the following Saturday and even plan to spend the night with the Ribolds. Jeff and Don would talk more about Annie and the past, and get better acquainted.

As they left, Don put his arms around Jeff and hugged him. "I still can't believe you are my grandson, after all these years," he said. "And actually, you are my oldest grandchild. Sophie has some grandkids, and my son, Marty, has two boys."

Jeff returned the embrace. "Good bye," he said, and took Carol by the arm to escort her to the car. "I'll see you next Saturday."

Chapter 8
FALL, 1969

Annie was energized by her new responsibilities in her job at the bank. She worked at typing the coding into the checks as they cleared the bank, and made periodic trips to the teller windows to pick up the checks received there for processing. The coding was a bit tedious, but she liked the people in the department. The supervisor was a little strict and unforgiving, but she was fair and treated everyone the same. Annie usually had lunch with Laurie in the employee cafeteria, enjoying a good meal for minimal cost. She figured she must have gained at least five pounds since she had started there.

Annie had called Carrie in September and found out that she had seen her brother, Marty, at a concert during the summer, and she was sure he was smoking pot. She wasn't sure if he had used anything harder. They laughed about Mr. Straight Guy, and how his parents would react to seeing him stoned. They caught up on the latest news in Green Meadow, as well as what was happening on campus. Annie told Carrie about her summer with Mark, her new job, and about her new friend, Laurie. They promised to keep in touch. And her good friend was sworn to secrecy about what was going on in Annie's life. Annie left no phone number or address, telling Carrie, "I'll call you."

She and Laurie would visit more and more frequently in the evening, usually in Laurie's apartment. Mark was gone so much, and Annie wanted the companionship. By late October, she had told Laurie more about her family and where they lived, and about her brother Marty. Her visits to Laurie's apartment usually involved some beer and marijuana. Laurie would turn on some Janis Joplin music, and sit next to Annie on the couch. They would share innermost secrets, both high with the effects of the alcohol and drugs. Their friendship was a source of comfort for both of them.

On Friday, Annie woke up feeling nauseous and made a quick trip to the bathroom. She lost whatever was left in her stomach, but felt better. She took a shower, combed through her hair, and fixed herself a piece of toast. Mark was sleeping. She had no idea what time he had come home last night, but she didn't want to wake him. She left him a love note on the table, and went on to work. About 10 AM, Annie felt nauseous again, and barely made it to the women's room to throw up. At noon, she told Laurie about getting sick.

"You haven't missed a period, have you?" Laurie asked.

Annie thought for a moment. "I didn't have a period last month. Do you think I might be pregnant? Oh, God, what would Mark say?"

"You'd better find out if you are pregnant. I've been to an OB-GYN here in town, and I'll give you the phone number." Laurie knew the answer would probably be positive. The question would be whether Mark would want to keep the kid.

Annie called and made an appointment for the next Tuesday to see the doctor. The weekend crawled by, as Annie contemplated how she would tell Mark about the pregnancy, if she was pregnant. She told him she had a touch of the flu, when he noticed her not feeling well. He fixed her some chicken noodle soup, and rubbed her back for her.

On Monday night, she shared her fears once again with Laurie. Laurie had the name of a guy who could arrange an abortion, if Annie wanted to end the pregnancy. Annie shuddered at the thought of going to someone for an abortion, having heard stories of infections and agony from such procedures. And it would be Mark's child.

On Tuesday, she finally had her doctor's appointment. She waited in the waiting room with about fifteen other women who were in various stages of pregnancy, or carrying around an infant. The receptionist had supplied her with a clipboard of forms to obtain information on her physical health and her ability to pay for the pregnancy and delivery. She struggled with some mixed emotions about having a child. Was she really ready to be a mother?

It was finally Annie's turn to be called into the doctor's area, behind the receptionist. The hallways were wide and decorated with a variety of paintings of women and children. The nurse led her into an examining room, where she directed her to remove her clothes and put on a gown that tied in the back. She left Annie there for some privacy. As Annie undressed, feeling very apprehensive about the examination, she noticed posters on the wall showing the stages of a child's development in the womb, along with the effect on various organs of the body.

The nurse returned to hand Annie a small cup, and directed her to the restroom to get a urine specimen. Then she took her blood pressure and got her weight on the office scales, making notes on a chart for the doctor. She directed her to a room and had her put on some white cloth leggings. Annie thought it was taking an eternity to get through all the preliminaries.

Finally, the nurse followed Doctor Torrey into the room. "Good morning, Florence," he said. "Do you go by Florence?" He smiled at her reassuringly.

"No, you can call me Annie," Annie replied, perched on the end of the examining table, where the nurse had instructed her.

"I understand you think you might be pregnant. We don't have the urine specimen test back yet, but I'm going to do a pelvic examination to see if we can tell for sure if you are pregnant. I'm going to ask you to lie back and put your feet in the stirrups of the table, then scoot all the way to the end of the table. I'll be very gentle and go slowly, Annie, so just try to relax." The doctor seemed conscious of Annie's anxiety.

Relax!? Annie thought. The examination took only a brief moment. The doctor also felt of her breasts, and then helped her sit up again on the end of the examining table. She didn't recall ever feeling so totally embarrassed. But she tried to remain calm.

"I'll be right back," Doctor Torrey said, and he walked back out of the room with the nurse.

"You can get dressed," the nurse told her as she closed the door. Annie quickly removed the gown and grabbed her own clothes to put them back on. Then she sat on the table and waited for what seemed like another eternity.

"Well, Annie, it looks like you are right. Everything indicates that you are, in fact, pregnant. From as near as I can tell, the baby will be born in May. I noticed that you are not married. Do you have some emotional support from the baby's father or from your parents to help you through the pregnancy and childbirth?" Doctor Torrey was concerned.

"I'll be fine, thanks," Annie said. "I have insurance through the bank where I work." The doctor talked with Annie about what to expect in the upcoming months as her fetus developed, then walked with her to the door that led back out into the reception room.

"Stop at the reception desk, and they will make you another appointment for next month. I'll want to see you every month at first, and then will see you more often later on in the pregnancy."

Annie felt really anxious. She would have to tell Mark, but what would his reaction be? And how did she feel about it? There was a real, honest to goodness baby growing inside her. Mark's baby. Annie went back to work for the remainder of the day, sharing again with Laurie the doctor's diagnosis. Laurie reassured her that she was there for her, no matter what Mark's reaction.

"You're what? You're pregnant?" Mark reacted to Annie's announcement when he came home for dinner. She had fixed him his favorite chicken dish.

"Yes. I was sick twice on Friday morning. Laurie had the name of a baby doctor, and I went there today to get an exam. He assured me that I am pregnant, with a baby due in May. Mark, what are we going to do?" Annie was still unsure of Mark's response.

"I'm going to be a dad! Yahoo, I'm going to be a dad!" Mark jumped up from his chair and pulled Annie to her feet. He grabbed her around the waist and lifted her into the air. "I'm going to be a dad!" he said again. "This calls for celebration!'

Mark grabbed a beer from the refrigerator and popped the cap. Then he looked into Annie's eyes. "Are you okay? Are you feeling sick now?" Mark was concerned.

"No, I'm okay right now. I'm just feeling a little full, and my boobs are sore, like when I'm about to start my period." Annie smiled at him. "Are you excited about this?"

"You bet I am. Annie Ribold, will you marry me?" Mark dropped to one knee and held her hand. "We can't let this kid come into the world without my name! We'll go to the courthouse as soon as we can and get married. What do you say?"

Annie was shocked. She hadn't even given a thought to getting married. She was just concerned about Mark wanting to keep the baby. "Yes, I'll marry you!" she said. Mark picked her up again and swung her around. He kissed her and held her close.

"We'll go to the courthouse in the morning. I think we have to get a blood test first, so I'm not sure we can get married tomorrow, but it will be as soon as possible. You and me, Annie. Mr. and Mrs. Mark Moss. I like it!"

They went to bed early that night and lay next to each other. Mark rubbed her abdomen and talked to the baby. He fondled her breasts and touched her to arouse her, pressing himself against her. They made quiet, peaceful love and fell asleep in each other's arms.

The next few days were a whirlwind, as they got their blood tests, arranged the marriage ceremony, and exchanged their vows at the courthouse. Laurie stood up with Annie, and the owner of the bar where they hung out stood up with Mark. Annie and Mark rode around town in a horse-drawn carriage and finally went back to their apartment. Annie could hardly believe her eyes, when she looked at the marriage certificate. Florence Ann Ribold Moss. She liked the sound of her new name, even if she had to put up with the first name. She loved Mark so much, and she was so happy that they were going to have this little family together. In just seven months, there would be three of them. Life was good. Winter and the holidays were just around the corner.

The holiday season started with Halloween in the apartment building. Annie and Laurie decorated the hallways for the youngsters who would be trick-or-treating there. They bought some candy, and sat together in the entrance foyer to pass out the goodies.

They each dressed in a witch costume, and painted their faces with white paint for effect, also wearing waxed white teeth. The kids were a little apprehensive about the two of them, but seemed to enjoy the fun.

Laurie and Annie also cooked for Thanksgiving Dinner, inviting a group of friends from the bar to join them. Laurie was a great cook, and she knew how to fix the turkey. Annie watched and wanted to learn so that she could do the same next year. Since they didn't have much room in the apartment, everyone sat on the couch, the floor, and even the steps outside the apartment to eat the delicious dinner the two of them had prepared.

After Thanksgiving, Annie decorated their small apartment for Christmas with some odds and ends she had picked up at the five and ten. They bought a small tree at a tree lot, and talked about beginning a tradition of tree decorating. Laurie came over to help pop some popcorn and make garlands for the tree, something her own parents had done years ago.

Annie was beginning to feel swollen and her pants and skirts were very tight around her tummy. Mark loved to rub her belly and talk to the baby. On Christmas night, Mark became serious as they were talking.

"Annie, I need to start getting a resume together and start looking for a real job. And I also need to get out of the drugs. The baby coming has made me look at things a little more seriously. I need to take care of you and the baby now, and be strictly legit. I'll figure out how to work it all out." He hugged Annie. "You are so beautiful! I'm the luckiest guy in the world."

Annie, Mark, and Laurie saw in the New Year, 1970, at the bar with their friends, after an evening at the movies to see *Butch Cassidy and the Sundance Kid.* Annie drank soda and stayed away from the pot. She couldn't risk any effect on the baby. They all walked back to the apartment at about 2 AM, Mark and Laurie stumbling along beside the very sober Annie.

Chapter 9
MARK, 1970

Mark read over his resume for any obvious errors. He had so many odd jobs over the years, even while he was still at the Home for Boys. But in college he had supported himself in ways other than legitimate jobs. At least he had the last six months at Readi-Warehouse. His boss had told Mark to use him as a reference. He looked at the responsibilities he had listed for the job, and knew that they wouldn't carry a lot of weight in consideration with an engineering firm. A friend at work had volunteered to help him put the resume together, and she had done as good a job with it as possible.

After work, Mark went to the library and made some copies of the resume and picked up some envelopes at the office supply store for mailing. On Sunday, he would check out the want ads for openings and get his resume sent out. With any luck, he would get an interview.

Since Annie had told him about the pregnancy, Mark had been elated with the thought of having a real family. Coming from a background of orphanages and boys' homes, he wasn't sure what it felt like to be a part of a family. He had watched the typical shows on TV that had involved the father, mother, and children, and it all seemed so surreal to him. Yet Annie was determined to stay away from her family, and didn't want to even contact them with news of the coming baby. Although he didn't totally understand Annie's animosity toward her parents, Mark knew that he loved her, and that the two of them would build their own family together. But along with the excitement over the baby, Mark knew it was time to settle down and get a real job, and to get himself out of the drug business as soon as possible. He had helped his contact get drugs moved through his job at the Readi-Warehouse, and it had been very successful. No one suspected that some of the boxes that came through his department were packed with products and a variety of drugs. Mark had devised a way to mark the drug shipments so as to be easily identified when the boxes reached their destination.

Mark's suppliers delivered drugs to his car during the day, and Mark would work late at night to move them into the designated boxes and load them on the truck. Each shipment resulted in an envelope with cash placed in his car for his role in the deliveries. The money had helped him pack away a serious amount of cash, as well as to have some extra spending money.

"Honey, I'm home!" Mark shouted as he came in the door. Annie hurried out of the kitchen to greet him with a hug and kiss. "Got anything cooked up for dinner? I want you to look at this resume to make sure I'm not missing anything. We'll go through the newspaper on Sunday to see what might be available."

"It's my treat out tonight. I got a small check today as a bonus, so I want to take you out to dinner. Let's go Chinese?" Annie was excited to be the one paying for once.

"Okay by me. You're getting to be quite a money-maker there at the bank. I always knew you were a smart one." Mark teased her. "I suppose you want to quit working to watch over the baby when it's born?"

"I'm not sure yet," said Annie. "I think about it sometimes when I'm really busy at work. I'll for sure stay home when he's first born until I have to go back, then I'll decide." Annie slipped on her boots while Mark steadied her on her feet, and then grabbed her coat, hat and gloves. "It's really cold out there today."

Mark's car was still warm from his drive home, so they got into the car to drive the three blocks to the Lonely Dragon. They enjoyed dinner and hot green tea before heading back to the apartment.

On Sunday, they poured over the want ads in the paper and found three positions for which Mark could send his resume. Annie made out the envelopes on the typewriter and typed up a short cover letter to include with the resume. She was excited for Mark to be applying for a job in engineering, as she knew he had been a good student at State. Annie knew that Mark was involved in selling drugs, and it made her more than a little nervous. She had heard stories about the Mafia and drug lords and the violence in the organizations. She was comforted by the fact that they were in a fairly small city, away from the big city crime syndicates. It would all be over as soon as Mark got a regular job. Annie dropped the resume envelopes in the mail on her way to work on Monday.

On Thursday evening the phone rang at the apartment. Annie took the message for Mark that he was to call a John Graham with Engineering Associates about the position he had applied for.

Mark called Mr. Graham on Friday, and they set up an interview for the next Monday afternoon. Over the weekend, Annie asked Mark questions that a prospective employer might ask to get him prepared for the interview. It hadn't been all that long since Annie got her job, so she could remember the kinds of things the bank employees asked her. Mark also gave her some hints on questions that related to engineering, so she could pose them as well. They decided Mark was ready for the interview.

The office of Engineering Associates was located on the other side of town from their apartment. Mark asked for a couple of hours off from his job to drive to the office for the interview. When he entered the building through the front doors, he put in his name with the receptionist and asked for John Graham. She handed him a clipboard with an employment application to complete, and motioned for him to sit in a straight-backed leather chair near the windows.

Mark quickly filled in the document and settled back to take in the surroundings. The walls were paneled in a dark wood, polished to a dull finish. The windows looked out into the street, now covered with snow and ice from the last storm. The leather chairs provided warmth in the room, along with the dark wooden tables covered with neatly stacked books on construction, architecture, and engineering. A water cooler stood by the hallway entrance. A fireplace flickered on the opposite wall with a painting of a fox hunt, framed with dark wood and hunter green matting, hung above the mantel. On the wall beside Mark a blueprint of the building was carefully drawn and lettered, while behind the receptionist a sculpture of copper, depicting a city skyline, filled the wall. Mark decided the firm had spared no expense in setting up the entrance area.

The phone rang on the receptionist's desk, and she smiled and nodded to Mark, "You can go in now. First door on your right down the hall. You can give John your application."

Mark stood up and walked the short distance to John's office door, noted by the brass name plate, and knocked. The door opened immediately; John had obviously been on his way out to greet Mark.

"Good afternoon, Mark. I've been expecting you. Sorry for the delay. I had a phone call I had to take. Please come in and have a seat." John extended his hand, and then led Mark to a chair beside a small table in a corner of his office.

"No problem. I had to fill in the application, and was really enjoying taking in the entrance to the building." Mark returned the gesture, and sat down where John had indicated.

The two of them discussed Mark's work experience and his time at Iowa State. John shared with Mark some of the work done in the office, as well as how many employees worked with him. He also described the entry-level position for which Mark had applied. He was curious as to why Mark had waited this long to look for a full time position in engineering.

"Mark, tell me why you went to work for Readi-Warehouse instead of looking for a job in engineering right out of college."

"Well, I had a chance at the job right away, and decided to take it until I could get settled here in Wahlberg. My wife and I have an apartment on the other side of town. She was also getting started in a job with the bank. We just got married a couple of weeks ago. So now I'm ready to really get my feet wet and get into my career." Mark hoped his explanation sounded adequate.

"Makes sense, I guess. I need to get this position filled as soon as possible. How soon could you get started here?" John seemed anxious to give Mark a chance.

"I think I could be on the job in two weeks, if that would be okay with you. I need to give notice at the Warehouse." *Among other things*, Mark thought to himself.

"Sounds good. I think we have everything we need on the application. On your first day on the job, you can fill in all the necessary paperwork for insurance and other benefits. I look forward to working with you." John stood and again extended his hand.

"Thank you for the opportunity. I'm not afraid to work hard, and I'll do a good job for you." Mark smiled and walked to the door. He looked back and said, "You don't know how much I appreciate this." He continued on down the hall, walking on air as he left the building.

Mark went back to work to finish out the day. He also had a shipment to work on later, so told his boss he would make up for his time off. He decided he would wait until the next day to turn in his notice. After most of the employees had left for the evening, he called Annie at the apartment.

"I got the job! I've got some things to finish up here that will take me a couple of hours, and then I'll be home. Put on that red teddy thing I like so well, and have the candles burning, Sweetie. See you soon." Mark was so elated, he could hardly contain himself. This was the beginning for him and for Annie, the beginning of a real life together. With his new job, they could start thinking of a house to rent instead of the apartment, especially with the money he had already stashed away.

Mark knew he had another call to make. His heart pounded in his chest as he dialed his supplier.

"It's Mark. I've got the stuff for today's shipment, but I need to tell you that I am walking away from this. I'm going legit and have a job waiting for me." Mark was almost breathless.

"What?! Mark, you can't just walk away. That's not what you do in this business. We are depending on you to get these shipments out for us, and we don't have an alternative. You'd better reconsider what you are doing. These guys don't mess around!" Mark didn't even know his name, but he was yelling on the phone.

Mark hung up the phone, with trembling hands. He had never been threatened like that before, as things had always worked smoothly with the shipments and his role in them. He stashed everything quickly into the boxes and loaded them on the truck. There was no turning back now. His mind raced to Annie and the baby. Did they know about them? He didn't remember ever telling his supplier that there were other people in his life. But they might have ways of finding out. He had to get home to Annie. He didn't want to worry her.

Annie met Mark at the door, but she could tell immediately that there was something wrong. Mark was white as a sheet, and was breathing as though he had run up several flights of stairs. "Mark, what is it?" Annie asked.

"It's nothing, Annie," Mark lied. "It's just that my drug supplier was pretty angry when I told him about leaving Readi-Warehouse, and it shook me up a little. But I'm here now, and it will all be fine when he has time to cool down. It will look a lot better tomorrow."

Annie got Mark a beer and rubbed his shoulders as he sat on the couch. "I'm so proud of you for getting that job!" she said. She kissed him and pulled the strap of her teddy down over her shoulder. "I think you had some plans for this evening, didn't you?" she asked, as she sat on his lap on the couch.

Mark kissed her bare shoulder. "And what are you going to do about those plans?" Mark was beginning to relax and could feel arousal with Annie's kisses.

Annie unbuckled his belt buckle, and unzipped his pants, reaching inside to stroke him. Then she helped him pull his pants down to his knees, and straddled him. "Since I don't have any panties on, and since you are tired from working all day, I'll just have to do all the work." She pulled her top over her head and tossed it aside.

Mark kissed her bare breasts and pulled her closer to him. "I've died and gone to heaven," he said, as Annie moved with him.

Later, as Annie slipped into a robe and warm slippers, Mark took her hand and led her into the bedroom. He opened the closet door and reached for a suitcase on the top shelf. He swung it onto the bed. When he opened it, Annie's mouth dropped open. The suitcase was filled with paper money.

"This is very heavy, Annie, so I want you to help me put it in some smaller bags. I want you to know about this, just in case anything should happen to me. I'm not telling you this to scare you, but I just feel better knowing that you know where it is."

They put the money into some backpacks and gym bags, and Mark lifted them back onto the closet shelves.

"Mark, you are scaring me," said Annie, a tear staining her cheek.

Mark brushed the tears away and lifted her chin. "Don't be afraid. Just know how much I love you and the baby. This is our nest egg for our little family." He kissed her and put his arms around her. Nothing in the world meant more to him than Annie.

On Tuesday, Mark was expecting another shipment from his supplier, and found the usual deposit and envelope in his car when he checked at the lunch hour. He stayed after work and boxed the drug shipment into the product boxes as he had done so many times before. He closed the doors of the truck, checked the locks on the building, turned out the lights, and walked back out to the car.

Mark reeled at the sound of someone following him as he neared his car. A man dressed in a black leather jacket was just behind him. Mark turned to make a break for the car, only to find that a second person was waiting for him there. Mark's blood turned cold as he saw the man nearest the car lift a baseball bat into the air. The bat caught Mark directly above his left ear and sent him sprawling to the ground. Mark tried to move, but couldn't. A second cut of the bat landed squarely across his back, and Mark thought he could hear bones breaking. The pain was excruciating. "Stop. Please!" cried Mark. But the two men were continuing their kicking and punching, until they finally started walking away. "You don't cross the boss, stupid!" That was the last sound Mark heard. He could feel his own warm blood trickling into his ear, but he couldn't move his head to stop it. Blackness overtook him. He couldn't breathe. Pain. Annie. The baby. "I love you Annie," he whispered.

The parking lot was dark. Ice sparkled as it caught the distant street lights. The car sat silently in the darkness, its driver lifeless by its side.

An hour later, a patrol car shined a search light across the parking lot, noticing the car parked there, and drove up to check it out. Not until the police officer was near the car did he see Mark's body, but immediately placed the call for an ambulance and assistance. The emergency team arrived too late.

Chapter 10
JEFF IN GREEN MEADOW

Jeff and Carol drove back to Green Meadow. Carol knew Jeff was deep in thought about his grandfather and what they had learned. They chatted superficially about the home and Sophie.

"What's next, Mr. Lipton?" Carol asked. She was curious as to what Jeff planned to do on Monday before he returned to Aubrey. "Will I see you tomorrow sometime?"

"I haven't even decided yet what I should do next. I'd like to drive up to Staley to see if I can locate Sandy Stahl, and I might try to run down my uncle Marty. Sounds kind of funny, doesn't it?" Jeff couldn't help but smile at the irony of now having an uncle to call by name. His discussion with Don Ribold had revealed a brother for Annie. "Sandy was good friends with Arlene Ribold, so she might have some ideas about those years when Annie was away from home."

"Sounds like a plan. I need for you to take me by the motel so I can pick up my car. Would you like to come by my house this evening? You could meet my mom." Carol wasn't anxious for the evening to end. She had a feeling that she would not see Jeff on Monday.

"I think I'll go back to the motel and call my folks. I haven't talked to them since Friday night, and I'm sure Mom will be concerned for me. Do you mind? And can I take a rain check?" Jeff reached for her hand and held it.

"No, I understand completely," said Carol.

"Carol, again, I can't thank you enough for everything you have done for me this weekend, and I will be in touch soon. Can you jot down your phone number for me so I can call you at home? I have the number at the restaurant."

Carol pulled out a small notebook from her purse, and wrote down her address and phone number in Green Meadow. She handed it to Jeff, who immediately tucked it into his jacket pocket. Having arrived in Green Meadow, Jeff pulled up next to the motel and Carol's car. Leaving the motor running, Jeff stepped out of the car as Carol came around. He reached for her arm and pulled her to him to kiss her gently, holding her closely.

"Good night, Carol. I'll be calling you soon." Jeff waited for Carol to get into her car and pull out of the parking lot.

He wondered how much had changed in this small town since Annie was there. He had noticed a gas station that had closed and was boarded up. Several buildings on the main street had various business signs above the doors, but they were empty and abandoned. A grocery store on one corner appeared to be a fairly new building, so Jeff wondered what might have been razed to make way for this new structure. What was there when Annie was in town?

One of the things Jeff wanted to see was the house that Annie had lived in when she was a girl. He didn't have the address for Don and Arlene's home in Green Meadow, but he could probably find it, or perhaps Don could give it to him on their visit next weekend.

Jeff's thoughts shifted to Don. He had seemed open and honest, but not particularly anxious to start talking about Annie. From what Jeff had heard about Annie at this point, there was probably some pain in those old memories, and Don wanted to get his wits about him as he gathered up information to share with Jeff. He seemed to be really happy with Sophie, and they certainly had a lovely home to share. Sophie had been a very good hostess, and she and Carol had enjoyed working on their supper together.

Carol. Blonde, blue-eyed Carol. Jeff smiled as he thought about her. She had this incredible take-charge attitude, and he knew she had enjoyed spending time with him. She wasn't at all pushy about the future of their relationship. Carol had just spent the better part of a weekend with him, but there was no obvious expectation for him to call her or even to come back to Green Meadow. Jeff found the mystery of Carol to be intriguing. There was no doubt he had to get to know her better. He had been so preoccupied this weekend. Any other woman would never want to see him again. But he was pretty sure Carol would be receptive.

As Jeff pulled into a parking space, it occurred to him that he might want to stop by the office and talk to Al at the motel to let him know where he had been the previous night. He was pretty sure Al kept tabs on his occupants.

"Hi, Al!" Jeff said, as he walked through the doors into the motel lobby. "Sorry I didn't call you last night. I was over in Chatsworth and ended up spending the night there. I'll be checking out in the morning."

Al studied Jeff for a moment. "I wondered what had happened to you. What have you been up to?"

The motel lobby was completely empty except for the two of them. Al was dressed in his usual black slacks and white shirt. "It's kind of a long story, but it's been a very interesting weekend." Jeff proceeded to fill Al in on his search for his family.

"You're Don Ribold's grandson? When I first laid eyes on you, I thought you looked somehow familiar. You really look a lot like him. Don was our insurance agent when I started working here. I saw him maybe once a year until he retired. Nice guy. Small world, isn't it?" Al beamed at Jeff.

"I still don't know the circumstances around my mother's death at such a young age. I hope to get more answers tomorrow. So if you'll excuse me, I'm going to hit the sack. I'll be checking out in the morning, and going back to Aubrey sometime tomorrow. See you then!" Jeff turned, and walked back out the front doors and down to his room.

The room had been carefully cleaned and freshened with new towels and glasses. The window coverings had been pulled back to open up the room to the pond out back, now hidden in the darkness. Jeff pulled the drapes and picked up the phone to call George and Sue.

Sue answered the phone. Jeff told her about finding Don Ribold, about Arlene Ribold having died of cancer, and about Sophie. He didn't mention Carol at this point, thinking it was too much to explain, and he was tired. Sue listened without comment, except to let Jeff know that she was listening. Jeff also told her that he would be seeing his grandfather again the next weekend. "Mom, you know I love you," he said, reassuring Sue that he had not forgotten her feelings. They said good-bye, with Jeff assuring her that he would be back in Aubrey to have dinner with Sue and George on Monday night.

Sue hung up the phone and turned to George. "He has found his grandfather, but Annie's mother is dead, and his grandfather has remarried. George, this is so hard. Just how much do you think he will discover about Annie, and what will he think?"

George put his arms around Sue. "We just can't worry about it at this point. Jeff is on the trail of information, and we will have to use discretion in listening to him and giving him guidance. Jeff knows we love him. I don't think that will change, no matter what the outcome. He is our son."

Jeff lay on the bed in his motel room, thinking about all the events of the weekend. Why didn't Don tell him more about Annie when he was there? Jeff didn't want to push him for information, but Don was definitely reluctant to talk about the past. Jeff thought he might call Don again in the morning just to say hello and to confirm their plans for next weekend. He was anxious to get to know him a little better.

He remembered the name Sandy Stahl from the breakfast at the restaurant on Saturday. They said she had moved to Staley. Maybe he would take a drive over there, and see if he could talk to Sandy. If she was good friends with Arlene, perhaps she could shed some light on Annie as well. Other than Sandy, Jeff decided that it might be better to wait to talk to others who might have known Annie and the Ribold family until he had a chance to talk more to Don. He looked at his notes. He had listed Sandy Stahl, Marty Ribold, and Jim Jarrett. But these were all people who were either in the family or knew the parents, not Annie. There must have been someone who was close enough to Annie to know more about her and her relationship with his father. If they left State to go east, where did they go? The news anchors on the TV droned on about the current events, but Jeff was lost in his thoughts. He switched off the television, and fell asleep.

In the morning, Jeff placed a call to Don Ribold. Don gave him the address of their home in Green Meadow, where Annie grew up, and Jeff made plans to meet him at his home on Saturday morning. Before driving around the town to see the high school, and to take one more trip out to the cemetery, Jeff went to the restaurant to have breakfast, but Carol was not working. He called her to see why she hadn't come in.

"My mom wasn't feeling well this morning, so I decided to stay at home with her. I'll talk to you later, okay?" Carol seemed distracted, and hung up the phone without saying good-bye, which caught Jeff by surprise. Women!

Chapter 11
ANNIE

Annie woke up and looked at the clock on the nightstand. It was 2 AM, and Mark wasn't home and in bed. She got up to go to the bathroom, washed her face, and looked at her reflection in the mirror. She looked tired, and she had dark circles under her eyes. Where was Mark? Annie put on her robe, and started for the door to the apartment to go to Laurie's, when there was a knock on the door that startled her.

Annie leaned her ear to the door. "Who's there? Did you forget your key?" she laughed.

"Ma'am, this is Detective Jenkins with the Wahlberg Police department. May we speak with you?"

Annie's heart stopped. The police? She opened the door just far enough for the chain to bridge the opening. One of the officers was dressed in uniform, the other in plain clothes with an overcoat and hat. The one identifying himself as Detective Jenkins held out his wallet with the badge and ID for her to see. Annie closed the door, slid the chain from the latch, and opened it.

"What is it? Is this about Mark?" Annie was very anxious.

"Ma'am, are you related to Mark Moss?" The detectives entered the apartment.

"Yes, I'm his wife. Has something happened to him?" Everything felt surreal to Annie. She felt as though she were watching a television show. It couldn't be real. Maybe she was dreaming?

"I'm afraid so, Ma'am. We are going to have to ask you to come with us. It appears that there has been an accident at the warehouse where your husband was working this evening, and he has been found dead." The officer extended his arm to catch Annie if she became faint.

Annie stared at him. "What? An accident? What kind of accident?" Annie's heart was pounding. Mark? Her Mark? There must be some mistake!

"Ma'am, we can talk more about this at the police station. Can I ask you to get dressed? If you will tell me where your coat is, I'll get that for you."

Annie moved like a zombie into the bedroom, took out some jeans and a sweater, slipped on shoes and socks, and walked back into the living room. The officer helped her into her coat, and she pulled her gloves out of the pockets and put them on. Tears were streaming down her cheeks uncontrollably. The officer handed her a handkerchief. He reached for her purse on the kitchen counter, and asked her if her keys were in it. Then the two walked her down the hall, down the stairs, and out into the cold night.

When they arrived at the police station, the officers escorted her into a room with a table and four chairs. The two of them were joined by a third man, who sat directly across from Annie.

"Would you give us your name, please?" the officer asked, and he clicked on a tape recorder.

"My....my name is Annie Moss, Florence Ann Moss." Annie was still sobbing into the detective's hanky, her eyes bloodshot from the flowing tears.

"Ma'am, we found your husband, Mark Moss in the parking lot of the Readi-Warehouse. It appears that he has been beaten to death. Is there anyone you can think of who might have done this to him?"

Annie thought about Mark and his concerns last night about his supplier. Her instincts told her that this was not the time to share this information with the officers.

"No, sir, I don't have any idea who might have done this. Mark works late occasionally at the warehouse."

"Annie, we have reason to believe that your husband may have been involved in some drug trafficking. There was an envelope in his jacket with some cash in it, and we found some drugs packed among the boxes on the truck that was being loaded on the dock. Can you shed any light on this for us?" Detective Jenkins was trying to be coy.

"You must be wrong about this. Mark would not be involved in drugs. He was going to be starting a new job in a couple of weeks." Annie wanted to emphasize Mark's innocence, but stopped short of mentioning her pregnancy.

"I'm afraid the evidence against him is pretty strong. There wasn't anyone else working there with him tonight. How much do you know about what he does at work when he is working late?" More probing questions.

"Detective Jenkins, would you mind if I go to the restroom? I'm not feeling very well." Annie tried to be calm, holding back her sobs.

"Sure, that's not a problem. The restroom is down the hall and on the right at the end of the hall. Just come on back here, so we can talk a little more, and then we'll get you back home." The officer was accommodating.

Annie picked up her purse and walked down the hall to the last hallway on the right. Just outside the door to the women's room, Annie noticed a pay phone mounted on the wall. She dug quickly into her purse to retrieve a quarter, and looked back down the hall to see if she had been followed. She dialed Laurie's number.

Laurie finally picked up on the third ring. "Hello?" she asked, sleepily.

"Laurie, I need your help. Are you awake?"

"I am now. What's up? Where are you?"

"I'm at the police station. Mark is dead. The police are suspicious of his involvement in drugs, and I think they also think I might be involved. I suspect there may be someone coming there to go through the apartment. Do you still have the key?" Annie was breathless, again looking back down the hall to see if anyone was coming.

"What?! Yes, I have the key. Annie, are you okay?"

"Just listen to me. Go to the apartment, and into our bedroom closet. Up on the shelves are some backpacks and two small suitcases. They are pretty heavy, so you might have to make more than one trip. Don't open them. I'll explain when I get out of here. Just please do this for me. We have to protect Mark."

"Okay, I'll do it. Annie, be careful."

Annie hung up the phone, again checked the hallway, and went into the ladies room. "Mark, my beautiful Mark," she said to her image in the mirror. The tears poured down her cheeks, and she sobbed uncontrollably.

A knock on the bathroom door startled her. "Ma'am, are you okay in there?" It was Detective Jenkins.

Annie opened the door, wiping her tears in the hanky. "Yes, I'm okay. She followed him down the hall and into the room. The walls were painted a dark taupe, with no window, no pictures, and a tile floor. An ashtray on the table was brimming with ashes, where the three of them had deposited their cigarettes.

"Annie, we just want to get to the bottom of all this. Did Mark ever talk about what he did at the warehouse when he stayed late?"

"No, sir. Mark never talked about his job there. There really wasn't much to talk about."

"Did you and Mark use drugs?"

The officers continued to ask Annie questions about Mark and how much she knew about his activities for some time. Annie was in shock at the thought of Mark's death. Yet she knew that she had to be very careful to not divulge her knowledge of Mark's activities, or to implicate herself in what had happened.

Finally, Annie asked Jenkins, "Can you take me back home now? I have a friend there at the apartments I can go to."

"I'll take you home. We can't do anymore here tonight. Annie, we had a search warrant issued, and some officers have probably already gone through your apartment to look for any signs of drugs. This is a serious investigation. Anything you can tell us will be helpful. We'd like to find the people who killed Mark. You understand?"

"Yes, I'll help in any way I can." Annie rose to leave the room. Detective Jenkins walked with her out to the police car, and drove her back to the apartment. He walked her up the stairs, and helped her with her key to the apartment. As soon as he had closed the door and walked away, Annie called Laurie.

Laurie held her as they sat together on the couch. "Oh, Annie, what can I say?"

"Laurie, I can't believe he's gone. What will I do? Did you get those bags out of here?"

"Yes, they're down in my apartment. You were right; there were some police here going through things. I saw them leaving with a couple of plastic bags full of stuff, but I don't know what they had. But, Annie, I'm worried about you. Are you okay?"

"I don't know. Can I stay with you tonight? I'm probably going to have to make some arrangements for a funeral for Mark. What about work? Laurie, I can't make it through all this without your help." Annie could feel the baby's movement and her thought went to the unborn child. "I have to take care of my baby." The tears boiled over in her eyes, and trickled down her cheeks once more.

"You know I'll be here for you. Let's go back to my apartment and get you to bed. I'll call in for you in the morning, and I'll take a vacation day so I can be here with you. We'll get through this, Annie, I promise." Laurie took Annie by the arm, grabbed her purse, and walked her down the hall to 2G. She helped Annie into her bed, and slept on the couch until the alarm went off at 7 AM.

Annie was still fast asleep when Laurie checked on her. She called her supervisor to tell her what had happened to Annie and Mark, and also that she might take off a couple of days to make sure Annie was okay. She would keep in touch.

The bags were locked with tiny padlocks, and Laurie wondered what was inside them that had concerned Annie so much. She knew her friend would tell her in due time. She found some space in a closet and stuffed the bags into it.

When Annie awoke and stumbled out into the living room, Laurie had fixed her some hot oatmeal and toast. Any expression of sympathy sent Annie into new tears, as her emotions were so frayed. She ate the oatmeal and drank a glass of milk. "Can we go to my apartment?" she asked Laurie. "I'm afraid I'll miss a call from the police or funeral home. They said they were taking Mark's body to the funeral home across from the park."

"Sure, let's go." They walked down the hall to Annie's apartment and opened the door to the ringing telephone. "Let me get that." Laurie wanted to protect Annie from whoever was on the phone.

"Is this the Moss residence? I'm Jason Jackson from the Wahlberg News, and I wanted to talk to Mrs. Mark Moss about his death last night?" Laurie looked at the phone in disbelief, and hung it back on the cradle.

"Annie, I'm afraid you are going to be getting some calls from some real cranks. Do you think you are safe here?"

"I think so. Mark never talked about drugs here at the apartment, so I doubt whether his supplier even knows I exist, unless somehow it gets out in the media. Do you think I'm in danger from the drug suppliers?" Annie was suddenly wary of danger.

"We need to protect you, Annie." Laurie was concerned. "You are welcome to stay with me until you feel a bit more comfortable in the apartment. If it's okay with you, I'm going to call Keith down at the bar, and see if he can help us out."

Laurie placed the call to Keith, who came right away to Annie's apartment. Keith went with Laurie and Annie to the funeral home, and helped them think through all the funeral arrangements. The three of them decided to keep Mark's obituary very brief, not mentioning Annie in the article. Since Mark was not aware of relatives he might have, there would be no need to publicize the funeral. His friends there in Wahlberg would be attending a very private funeral, with no visitation.

The Readi-Warehouse personnel office called to let Annie know what she would have to do to claim on life insurance and how to collect Mark's last check.

At around 4 PM, there was a knock on the apartment door. "Mrs. Moss, this is Detective Jenkins again. May I come in?"

Annie, Laurie and Keith all looked at each other. Annie got up to open the door for the detective.

"Annie,... may I call you Annie?" he paused. "Annie, we found some minor indications of drugs in your apartment, but we are not going to arrest you for this. We do believe that your husband was involved with the transfer of drugs through the warehouse. If you have any information that might lead us to these people, please let us know. We'd like nothing better than to put them behind bars for Mark's death, and to stop the flow of drugs in this area. Are you going to be alright?"

"I'll be fine, thank you." Annie smiled at the detective, who tipped his hat and left the room, leaving Annie, Laurie and Keith in a few moments of silence.

"Do you know anything, Annie?" Keith asked.

"No, I really don't. Mark was concerned last night, because he had told them he wanted out, that he was going to a real job in engineering and would be leaving the warehouse. He said the supplier had yelled at him, and he was pretty nervous about it. I can't believe they beat him to death. What kind of people would do something like this? Someday, I'll find out who did this to Mark." Annie was angry. "I promise you that."

Chapter 12
JEFF

Jeff drove around Green Meadow, noting where his mother may have been when she was a young woman growing up in the town. He drove by her house, and then drove out to the cemetery to see her grave again. The sun was shining and the cemetery was much pettier than he had remembered it from Friday. The sun shone on Annie's stone, warming the surface of the marble. Jeff noted that there were some flowers in the vase on the side of her headstone that hadn't been there on Friday. He would ask Don about them. "Annie, I have a feeling there is more to your life than what I have found out so far. I wish you were here to talk to me. If there are people who know your story, I'll find out. Good-bye for now." Jeff stood and walked back to his car.

The drive to Staley took about forty minutes, as Jeff drove through the country roads to get there. The processing plant was on the west side of town, and Jeff could see the tower as he drove through on the state highway. Staley reminded him a lot of Aubrey, with wide streets and neatly mowed lawns. Most yards had mums still in bloom, and pumpkins, corn shocks, and various colors of gourds decorated porches and front lawns. The houses were built mostly of brick and siding, with only a few that were the older, two-story homes so often seen in these small communities. The administrative building of the plant was set back from the street on a grassy knoll behind a lake with a fountain that sprayed water into the air. The cool autumn breeze blew the water to create a misting effect for the cascade. A few ducks swam near the edges of the pond, and trees were planted in perfect order around the park-like setting. Jeff thought the person who had created this must have been very talented. He pulled through the circular driveway to the visitor parking lot and turned off the ignition. He wasn't sure if Sandy Stahl would want to talk to him, but he was going to give it a try. It was getting close to noon.

"My name is Jeff Lipton. I wonder if I might see Sandy Stahl." Jeff introduced himself to the receptionist. He noted the tall windows and view from the front desk. A large framed canvas behind the receptionist held a map of the United States with various pins in locations where the company was doing business.

"I'll try Sandy for you." The receptionist dialed an internal number. "Sandy, a young man named Jeff Lipton is here to see you." She turned to Jeff. "She will be right out."

Sandy Stahl was dressed in black slacks and an orange blouse with a vest decorated with embroidered pumpkins, bats, and witches for the Halloween season. Despite her obvious interest in keeping with the season, she appeared very professional and in control as she extended her hand to Jeff. "Good morning, I'm Sandy Stahl. How can I help you, Jeff?"

"Sandy, I understand you were good friends with Arlene Ribold when the two of you worked together here? I've been doing some family research and wanted to ask you a few questions about Arlene and her daughter, Annie, if you might have a few minutes." Jeff wasn't sure what her reaction would be.

"Tell you what. It's a nice day. I'll go grab my sandwich and an iced tea, and we can visit while I eat my lunch. Would that be okay with you?" Sandy was matter-of-fact, and seemed open to talking with Jeff.

"Sure, where shall I meet you?"

"Just stay right here, and I'll be back in a few minutes." With that Sandy was back through the doors to the right of the reception desk, and out of sight. She returned in about five minutes with her lunch and her iced tea, and motioned for Jeff to follow her out the side door and around to where there were some tables set up for employees to enjoy lunches and breaks.

"Let's sit here." Sandy pointed to a table in the sun. "It's a bit chilly to sit in the shade." They sat down at the table, and Sandy opened her lunch sack. "Tell me what this is all about, Jeff. Arlene and I were very good friends."

Jeff proceeded to tell Sandy about his search for his natural mother, about finding Annie's grave, and about his meeting with Don Ribold. Sandy listened without uttering a word, taking an occasional bite of her sandwich and a sip of her drink.

"I don't know what to say or where to start, Jeff. You have obviously already found out that there was a lot of friction between Annie and Arlene. Arlene blamed herself that Annie didn't get back in touch with her until the end. She was always looking forward to the day that Annie would come back home, and that they would be able to work things out. I thank God that my son didn't get involved in the drugs and other things that were going on then. He was the same age as Annie, and they graduated together from Green Meadow High." Sandy looked at Jeff. "I can't believe you are Annie's son. But you sure do have some resemblance to Don and to Annie."

"Others have told me that as well," said Jeff. "Can you tell me anything about Annie's death and others who may have known her?"

"When Annie went off to State, she roomed with Carrie Bloom. Carrie's mom still lives in Green Meadow and I think works for the city there. After Annie left, Carrie never let on that she knew where Annie was, but Arlene always thought she really did. One day, out of the blue, the Ribolds got a call from a hospital out east that Annie was asking for them and that she was in serious condition. Arlene was on a plane and with Annie the next day, but Annie died shortly after her arrival. Arlene wouldn't talk about her cause of death, and there were some rumors, but I don't think anyone knows the whole story. Maybe Don will know more. The good thing was that she and Annie had a chance to make peace before Annie died. Arlene was a wreck after the funeral. But she eventually managed to go on after that and kept working up until the time she was diagnosed with breast cancer. Arlene was a great friend, and I still miss her. She's been gone a long time already. Have you met Sophie?" Sandy was curious.

"Yes, I have. I haven't had a chance to talk much to Don yet, but we are meeting next Saturday, and he's going to give me more of Annie's things and tell me what he knows about her death." Jeff smiled at Sandy. "You don't know how much I appreciate you sitting with me and sharing what you know."

"I'm glad to help out. How did things work out for you with your adoptive parents?"

"George and Sue Lipton adopted me, and Mom gave me a copy of the adoption papers, my birth certificate, and some other things from Annie. They have been really good to me, and I plan to be back tonight to have dinner with them." Jeff walked Sandy back to the front of the building and shook hands with her again. Although he hadn't planned to go back through Green Meadow, he decided to make another trip to talk to Carrie's mother. Carrie might be his best resource.

As Jeff drove back to Green Meadow, he thought about what he already knew about Annie. She had evidently been very rebellious as a teenager and, maybe because of the use of drugs, had alienated her parents. She had gotten herself into a bad situation, leaving college and running off somewhere. He felt some comfort in the fact that she had seen her mother before her death, but wondered why then? What was missing were all those years between the time she left college and the phone call that was made to the Ribolds. Sandy had referred to the rumors around Annie's death, and Jeff wondered what those were. The afternoon sun shone in Jeff's window as he drove west back to Green Meadow. He pulled up outside the city building, where he and Carol had visited on Saturday.

"Remember me?" Jeff asked Sally Coates, as she met him at the counter.

"Yes, I remember you. What can I help you with now?" Sally smiled at him.

"I'm looking for Mrs. Bloom. I believe she is Carrie Bloom's mother. Carrie was Annie Ribold's roommate in college, and I'd like to see if she can give me Carrie's address and phone number."

"Wait just a minute. I'll see if Jennie is in the office. She works downstairs in the permits department." Sally dialed a number on the phone and talked briefly to the person on the other end. In a few minutes, a rather portly lady came through the doorway at the back of the office. She wore her hair in a 70s hairstyle, with the top of her hair teased. Her glasses were attached to a black cord, draped around her neck. The dress she wore was long and swayed back and forth with her movement as she walked toward the front counter.

"Jennie Bloom, this is Jeff Lipton. He's doing some research on the Ribold family, and wanted to know if you have Carrie's address so that he could contact her about Annie." Sally motioned to Jeff.

"Well, I don't suppose there's any harm in giving you Carrie's phone number. She lives in Minnesota now. She married a Slater, and he's a veterinarian there in Chatham." Jennie took a small notebook out of her pocket and opened it. "Her address is 1421 E. Caldron, and her phone number is area code 299 376-9999. She and Annie were good friends and went to college together. But I think they lost contact when Annie left school back in '69. Carrie didn't say much about Annie after that." Jennie started toward the back door, and then turned back to Jeff. "You tell that Carrie, if you talk to her, to call her mom!" Jennie shook her finger at Jeff.

Jeff had written down all the information from Jennie. "Thanks, I'll do that," he called after her as she walked briskly away. He thanked Sally for her help, and walked back to his car to make the trip back to Aubrey for dinner with his mom and dad.

When Jeff arrived at his parents' home, he walked in the back door and into the kitchen. Sue was there preparing dinner. Jeff could smell the aroma of his favorite casserole baking in the oven. Sue was working on a salad, chopping celery and carrots when he came in.

"Hi, Mom," he said and kissed her on the cheek. "Dad home yet?"

"No, I look for him any minute though. Go ahead and get washed up, and you can help me set the table." Sue was glad to see Jeff back at home.

"Always trying to give me work to do! Such a deal!" Jeff walked out of the kitchen, down the hall, and into the bathroom to wash his hands. He met up with a small gray and white cat on his way, giving her some attention.

"Hey, I met a really neat gal in Green Meadow. She works at the restaurant where I ate dinner on Friday night. She helped me out quite a bit, and even drove to Chatsworth with me on Saturday." Jeff was anxious to tell his mom about Carol, and smiled thinking of her. "I'll tell you all about her and our discoveries when Dad gets here."

When George came home, they all sat down to dinner. Jeff told them all about Carol and what the two of them had found out. He described Don Ribold and Sophie to them, and also told them about Sandy Stahl and his conversation that afternoon. Sue and George listened intently to Jeff, neither of them saying much as he related his weekend. Jeff was so wrapped up in his own thoughts that he wasn't aware of their silence. After dinner, he helped Sue carry the dishes and load them in the dishwasher. Then he left for his own apartment, telling them he would keep in touch, and reminding them that he loved them.

Jeff was anxious to get back home. It was on the ground floor of an apartment complex on the east side of town, settled among some upscale housing being built in the area. The outside of the buildings were brick and had ample windows on the exposed sides. Each apartment had a deck large enough to do some entertaining in the summer months, and a fireplace for ambiance in the winter.

Jeff's apartment had two bedrooms, one of which he was using as an office. He hadn't had much interest in decorating the walls with paintings, but had a few things hanging that he had acquired over time. Sue had helped him pick out the drapes and covers for his bed, so they would match. The walls were all painted ivory, and the compact kitchen had a horse-shoe shaped counter, a refrigerator, a gas-burner stove, and a dishwasher.

As Jeff unlocked the door and opened it, his long-haired black and white cat Molly ran to the door to greet him. She purred and rubbed against his leg. Jeff would have to be sure to thank the neighbor for looking in on Molly and feeding her. He dropped his keys on the kitchen counter, threw his jacket on the chair in the living room, and kicked off his shoes. He carried his suitcase back to the bedroom, and popped the latches to open it. Molly followed him from room to room, until he finally took the time to really pet her. In the bedroom, she hopped up on the bed and sniffed the contents of the suitcase. "Can you smell another woman in there?" Jeff laughed at Molly.

He walked back to the living room and clicked on the TV. The evening programming was already in progress. He reached into his shirt pocket and found the phone number that Carrie's mother had given him that afternoon. He dialed the number. One ring, two rings, and then...

"Hello?"

"My name is Jeff Lipton. May I speak to Carrie?"

"This is Carrie."

"Carrie, I'm doing some research on my family ancestry, and I understand you knew Annie Ribold, is that correct?"

"Yes, Annie was my roommate in college, and my dearest friend. What does that have to do with you?"

"I don't know how else to start into this, except to tell you that I have recently discovered that Annie Ribold Moss was my mother. I have found her dad in Chatsworth, but haven't yet had much time to visit with him. Sandy Stahl, who was a good friend of Arlene Ribold told me about you, and your mother gave me your address and phone number." Jeff paused. There was silence on the phone. "Are you there?" Jeff asked.

"Annie had a child? I don't believe it! She never told me." Carrie seemed offended, and even angry at the revelation. "Jeff are you absolutely sure about this?"

"Yes, I am. I have the birth certificate and her signature on my adoption papers. Short of some kind of blood test, I think there is no doubt." Jeff paced the floor with his remote phone.

"What do you want from me?" asked Carrie. "Annie and I kind of lost touch, obviously, since I didn't know she had a child."

"I would appreciate anything you can tell me about Annie and about my father. I'd like to find people who knew her in New York. Do you know anyone by name?" Jeff was hoping she could throw some light on that time period.

"Annie called me a few times after she left school. She told me that she and Mark had gotten married, and then she called to tell me that he had died, and that she was alone. She was working in a bank there. She finally gave me her phone number in case I needed to get hold of her." Carrie was beginning to share some information with Jeff. "There was a friend she talked about named Laurie, but I don't know the last name. I got the impression they were really good friends."

"When was the last time you talked to Annie?" Jeff asked.

"Gosh, I don't even remember. I gave her phone number to Marty once when he called, really anxious to get hold of Annie, but the next thing I knew, Mom called to tell me that Annie had died in Wahlberg, New York. Do you know the circumstances around her death and what happened to Mark?" Now Carrie was asking the questions.

"That's what I'm trying to find out. I keep getting little bits and pieces of information and am trying to find the answers for myself. If I give you my phone number, would you call me if you think of anything that might be helpful?" Jeff could tell that Carrie had told him everything she could remember at the moment, still in shock at Jeff's announcement.

"I sure will, Jeff."

"Did you know my father?" Jeff held his breath at the question, waiting for her response.

"Of course, I knew Mark. He and Annie started seeing each other during the second semester of our freshman year. She was madly in love with him, Jeff, and I am sure the feeling was mutual. Once they started seeing each other, they were inseparable. When Mark asked her to go away with him, there was no doubt in Annie's mind. She wanted her life to be with him. She swore me to secrecy and promised to call me, but I never knew exactly where she was. I wish I could tell you more."

Jeff smiled slightly at the thought of his mother being so in love with Mark. "Thank you Carrie. Oh, by the way, your mother said you should call her. I'm just relaying that message at her request."

"Thanks for the reminder. We just get busy, you know? Good-bye for now, Jeff, and good luck to you. Maybe I'll get to meet you sometime when I'm back in Green Meadow. I'd like that." Carrie hung up the phone.

Jeff looked at the phone for a moment, and then placed it back in the charger. His father's name was Mark. Annie's friend's name was Laurie. Another name, a place, and another fragment of information.

Chapter 13
ANNIE

Annie did not attend the graveside rites for Mark. Keith and Laurie insisted that she stay away to protect her identity from anyone with whom Mark might have been involved. Annie felt emptiness so overwhelming that she thought she would never recover.

The baby was getting more active by the day, and Annie slowly began to turn her focus toward the baby. She stayed with Laurie for some time, but returned to work. At least with Laurie and with Keith's constant attention, she felt less lonely. She shared with Laurie the contents of the bags, and on her insistence, emptied them into safe deposit boxes at the bank. Laurie signed the cards with Annie and took a key, in case anything ever happened to Annie. In the meantime, Annie would have the money available to her if she needed it for the baby.

The three of them worked through the winter months. Annie kept busy with her job, and she finally returned to her own apartment, determined to make a home for herself and the baby when the time came. She and Laurie shopped for baby furniture and clothes, and Laurie held a shower for her, inviting co-workers and friends. By the time the baby was due to be born, Annie's apartment looked like it was more for the baby than for her.

On Saturday, Annie awoke in damp sheets, and felt the first of the contractions. She called Laurie in a panic. "I think the baby is coming. My water broke! Can you come over?"

Laurie sat up in bed. "I'll be right there!" She slipped into her jeans and a sweatshirt, grabbed her socks and loafers and bolted down the hall to Annie's apartment.

Annie let her in, holding her abdomen. "The pains aren't too bad yet, and I haven't had a chance to time them." Annie's eyes were wide with anticipation. "I'm supposed to call the doctor as soon as I know for sure I'm in labor, but he also wants to know how far apart the pains are." She walked to her bedroom and started to lay out some clothes to put on, when the next pain came.

Laurie marked the time, and then braided her hair as she waited for the next one. Annie quickly dressed and ran a brush through her hair. They called the doctor's number to relay the information, grabbed Annie's hospital bag, and Laurie helped her walk carefully down the stairs to the first floor and out to her car.

The trip to the hospital was short, and they got Annie into the emergency room for admission. The doctor had already called ahead and the staff was ready for her. They put her into a wheelchair and started off for the baby delivery area. The nurses gave Laurie instructions as to where she could wait for news from her friend. She called Keith, who came right away to wait with her.

After what seemed like an eternity, and many cups of coffee, the doctor came out to tell Laurie and Keith that Annie had delivered a baby boy, and that both were doing fine. They hugged each other and beamed with excitement over Annie's new baby.

"Annie is resting right now, but you can see the baby if you like. He's in the viewing area down the hall and to your right. We'll have all the stats on him in Annie's room in a little while. You are welcome to go in to see her, but you might want to make your visit short tonight. We'll send her home in a couple of days. I'd appreciate it if one of you could be here to take her home. Do you know if she will have some help for a few days?" The doctor knew of Mark's death and that Annie was alone.

"Annie will have all the help she needs," Laurie said. "All of us will take turns giving her a hand until she is ready to take the little guy on for herself." Laurie laughed. "She'll probably be ready to kick us out!"

When they peeked in on Annie, she was almost asleep. "He's beautiful, Laurie!" Annie said.

"We just saw him, and you are absolutely right. He's perfect. We just wanted to let you know we were still here, and I'll come back to see you tomorrow. You get some rest now, okay?" Laurie patted her arm and gave her a reassuring hug. "It's all going to work out fine, Annie. You'll be a terrific mom."

Annie decided to name the baby Jeffrey. She had always liked the name, and it just seemed to fit him. She would call him Jeff. The nurses helped her learn how to feed and bathe the baby, and gave her a few other tips on how to deal with crying. By the time Annie was ready to go home, they had supplied her with all sorts of diapers, bottles, bibs, and formula. Laurie helped her get all the supplies into the apartment and get settled.

Jeff was a good baby. He seemed content with the formula, and grew very quickly. Annie stayed home for the allotted six weeks before returning to work, and it was very hard to leave him the first time with Mrs. Sheldon in Apartment 1C. The sitter had come highly recommended by someone else in the apartment building. Mrs. Sheldon had kept her child as an infant until about four years old, and had done a wonderful job. Laurie and Annie worked it out so that Annie went in to work late and came home later, and Laurie went in to work early, returning to pick up Jeff. He spent less time at the sitter that way, and Laurie loved keeping him until Annie got home.

Annie managed to keep her apartment, take care of Jeff, and meet her own needs with her salary. She had gotten an increase in pay and a promotion to a new responsibility at the bank, and she had health insurance for herself and the baby.

Whatever Annie, Keith and Laurie planned, Jeff was part of the activity. Annie bought a big stroller so she could take him almost anywhere. They spent a good deal of time outside in the summer months, taking Jeff to the park and on walks around town. The four of them were practically inseparable, when they weren't at work.

One evening when Annie was walking alone along the bike path in the park, pushing Jeff in the stroller, she was startled to hear a cyclist call her by name as he passed. It took a moment to recognize him, but she finally realized it was Detective Jenkins, who had interviewed her when Mark died.

"Hello, Annie. I'm not sure if you remember me. I'm Jack Jenkins, from the police department. We met last winter in less than pleasant circumstances." He paused, waiting for Annie to comment. "I want to apologize if I was a bit hard on you during the interview. We just weren't sure of your involvement in the whole situation."

"Yes, I remember you. As you can see, there have been some big changes in my life since Mark's death."

"Is this your baby? I didn't realize you were pregnant. Congratulations! Boy or girl?"

"Boy. His name is Jeff." Annie wasn't interested in getting into much of a conversation with him.

"Annie, I just want to say, we are still looking for the people responsible for your husband's death. There is still a lot of drug dealing going on here in Wahlberg, and we just can't seem to get our arms around it. It's very frustrating. I was concerned for your safety, but am going to assume you were not threatened?" Annie didn't hear his concern as much as she heard the question.

"I didn't know anything then, and I don't now, Detective Jenkins. Believe me, if I knew who had beaten Mark, I'd be out there myself trying to find them. My baby has to grow up without a father because of them. But thanks for your concern." Annie was abrupt.

"I understand, Annie. Remember that if you ever run across these guys, give me a call. It would be my pleasure to bring them to justice. Good to see you again, and take care of that little guy." He nodded at Annie, and then rode off on his bicycle.

Annie felt nauseous at the thought of Mark's death. She had put it out of her mind as she cared for Jeff, but the sight of the detective had brought it all back. Annie felt anger burning inside her. They had taken her Mark away from her, and from their baby. They had beaten him to death and left him on the icy pavement of a deserted parking lot. Annie felt a cold shiver as she felt the first cool air of the approaching fall season blow against her cheek. She reached down to cover Jeff's arms in the stroller, and hurried back to the apartment.

Laurie and Annie would often take Jeff with them to the bar to see Keith, and have a beer. Jack Jenkins came by the bar sometimes and would join them. He became a regular and often joined their table of friends when he wasn't on duty. Annie thought he was a totally different person when he wasn't on duty. He seemed to even take a liking to Jeff, often holding him when he would get fussy and bouncing him on his knee. Jeff would giggle at the diversion.

Annie would occasionally call Carrie to see what was happening back in Green Meadow. She had told her that Mark had died, but didn't go into details. She always stopped short, however, of telling her about Jeff. She had a feeling that Carrie would get on her to contact her parents, and she didn't want to get into that with her. She had her own family now in Wahlberg. Carrie told her that Marty had gone to a small college in New York City, and she was pretty sure he was really getting into the drugs. He didn't go back to Green Meadow much, and most of his friends were gone. She also told Annie about her plans after graduation, and asked if Annie would give her a phone number so they wouldn't lose each other. Annie agreed, making Carrie promise not to give the number to her parents if they asked for it. "Annie, I really wish you would get over this and make contact with them. I know they all love you and want you to come home." Carrie was frustrated with Annie's attitude. She felt that Annie really would like to get in touch, or she wouldn't be so curious about what was going on. But Annie was her friend. She had no intention of driving her away. After graduating and moving to Minnesota, Carrie had called Annie to give her the new phone number, but they did not discuss Annie's family affairs.

Both Annie and Laurie were given promotions at the bank over time, taking on more responsibility. Annie even considered the possibility of returning to school to get some more of her education. She and Jeff had gotten into a good routine of work and play, and he thoroughly enjoyed time with Laurie and Keith as well. Jack Jenkins had taken Annie to a movie a few times and out to dinner. Annie had grown to like Jack, but she wasn't anxious to get involved with another man. She was still mourning Mark and felt she would always love him. Little Jeff was all the man she needed in her life at the moment.

When Jeff was nearly four, Annie started to look at where she was going to send him for kindergarten. A local church had a pre-school program, and Annie enrolled Jeff there, to be sure he had the skills needed for kindergarten. He seemed to be doing well, and got along with the other boys and girls. He and Annie spent a lot of time reading books, especially on cold winter nights.

One night, Annie got a phone call that would change her life. "Annie, this is Marty. I'm in some serious trouble."

Chapter 14
MARTY

Annie nearly dropped the phone. "What? Marty? How did you get my phone number?"

"I called Carrie and told her it was an emergency. She gave it to me, but made me promise not to give it to Mom and Dad. Sis, I need some help."

"Where are you? What can I do?" Annie was taken completely by surprise with the call. Her mind was racing in anticipation of Marty's answer to her question.

"I've been arrested. It's a long story, but I've really screwed up. I need some help to get out of jail, but more than that, I need help to get myself out of a big mess." Marty went on to tell Annie that he had been using drugs, and had been selling drugs for a supplier. The police had confiscated his drugs and he wasn't going to be able to deliver on the money to his supplier, even if he did get out of jail. He was crying as he told Annie how frightened he was.

"Give me a number where I can reach you. I need some time to think! I'm not sure what I can do. How much is the bail?" Annie's mind was again flooded with thoughts of Mark. She had no choice but to try to help Marty.

Marty gave her the phone number at the police station in New York, and told her the bail had not yet been set. He again pleaded with her to help him, as she was his only hope. He couldn't tell their parents what was going on.

"Just keep cool, Marty. I'll see what I can do. I'll call you as soon as I know something." Annie hung up the phone and stared at it for an instant. Then she picked up the phone and dialed Jack Jenkins.

"Jack, this is Annie. Can you come over to my apartment? I need your advice on something, and I don't want to talk about it on the phone."

"Sure, I'll be right over. Is Jeff okay?"

"Yes, he's in bed already. I'll put on some coffee, but come as quick as you can." Annie went to the kitchen, her hands trembling. She filled the carafe with water, and poured it into the coffee maker, adding the coffee to the filter, and then clicking on the switch. It occurred to her that she was walking in a dream, performing tasks like a robot.

Within fifteen minutes, Jack was knocking at her door. She let him in and motioned for him to follow her to the kitchen, where she poured him a cup of coffee. "Cream and sugar?" she asked.

"No, I'm good. What's up?" Jack was anxious to hear what had Annie so upset.

"I just got a phone call from my brother, who I haven't talked to in almost six years. He got my number from an old college friend. Marty called from a police station, Jack. It sounds like he's involved in using and selling drugs, and he is really in a jam." Annie proceeded to tell Jack about her conversation with Marty, and how frightened Marty was. "As you can imagine, it brings back memories of Mark."

"Annie, will you let me get involved in this? I need to do some checking, and I don't want to get my hopes up, but this might be an opportunity to get our hands on some of these guys. Jack looked at Annie. "Do you think we could bring Marty to Wahlberg?"

"What are you talking about?" Jack had lost her.

"If this is the same source that was supplying Mark at the Readi-Warehouse, then they must have a cell here as well. But I need to do some research on some things. In the meantime, I'll get in touch with the police through this number you have for Marty, and get them involved. At some point, I'll need for you to help me talk to Marty. Annie, can you do that?" Jack was holding her hand, pleading for her cooperation.

"I don't want to lose my brother the same way I lost Mark!" Annie was upset with him, and started pacing the floor. "We can't risk that, Jack!"

"Let's just wait and see what we can work out. I'll place a call tonight to the police station, and have them hold off for 24 hours until we can get a plan in place. Just give me a little time, Annie."

"I don't have any choice, Jack. I don't know what I can do for him. This is like a nightmare." She turned on her heel to face him. "Okay, call me tomorrow and let me know what is happening. I'll call in sick tomorrow at the bank, and be here waiting for your call." She let Jack hold her for a few fleeting moments, and then pulled away.

Jack finished his coffee, grabbed the coat he had thrown over the recliner, and left the apartment. Annie slipped on her pajamas, turned out the lights, and sat in the darkness. Tears streamed down her face as she thought of Mark's last night with her. He was afraid, much the same as Marty, and he paid for his mistakes with his life. Now Marty was in trouble. She wasn't even sure she would recognize him, it had been so long. And he had grown up in that time. The anger she had felt toward Mark's killers was renewed, and she clenched her fists. If there was anything she could do to help them catch the guys who had killed Mark, she would do it.

Then she thought of Jeff. She walked into his bedroom, her way lighted by the street lamps outside Jeff's window. What if anything ever happened to her? Who would take care of her little Jeff? She brushed his dark curls away from his forehead and kissed him there. He had kicked off his blankets, so she pulled them back up over his shoulders. Around the room, Jeff had accumulated books, toys, games, and stuffed animals. A group of toy soldiers stood in formation along his window sill. She tucked Charlie Bear under the covers with Jeff.

Annie went to bed, but slept only fitfully for the rest of the night, her sleep interrupted by haunting memories. She would fill Laurie in on what was going on in the morning.

Marty sat in the small cell at the police station. He was sharing the space with someone who was quite drunk and snoring loudly on the bunk across the room from his own. His mind was full of the events of the night; the raid, the arrest, and the trip to the police station. Would Annie be able to help him? He wasn't sure what Annie's life was like now. He knew only that she had left college to run off with some guy who had graduated. He also knew that Annie had been using drugs in high school and college.

Marty had heard of the fate of people who had crossed the suppliers. His blood ran cold at the thought of being shot or beaten by thugs. Everything had worked so well for him up until now. He had an outlet for his supply of drugs, and he had a good relationship with the person who made the drops and pickups. But now, since the police had his supply and the money he had collected, he would not be able to turn it over. He choked on a sob, as he considered his situation. What if he had to go to jail? What would that do to his parents? Would they disown him when they found out? Marty was getting more and more anxious as the effect of the drugs was wearing off, and he was more in touch with reality. His hands were trembling, and nausea came over him. He could kill for a hit about now.

Chapter 15
JEFF

Jeff woke up early on Tuesday morning. He showered and dressed quickly, grabbed a cup of coffee and a donut on his way to work, and had some time to look over his desk before other employees started to arrive.

"How was your trip? Everything turn out okay?" Gary Olsen asked. Gary was in his late 60s and was beginning to show a little gray at the temples. Jeff admired him for his physical condition, slim and muscular with just the right weight for his height. Slightly shorter than Jeff, Gary was always dressed in business casual, seldom wearing a tie, except if he had to travel to a special meeting or attend the local Rotary luncheon. Gary extended his hand to greet Jeff.

"Well, it seems I have more questions than answers at the moment. I found my birth mother's grave, and have located her father in Chatsworth. I'm going to see him again next weekend. But I haven't yet found the explanation for her early death, nor why I was placed for adoption. Everyone I talk to gives me another name, and another lead. The last one I heard, when I called a college roommate, was that she lived in Wahlberg, New York. That's a long ways away from Iowa!" Jeff walked to the coffee maker and pressed the tap to get another cup of coffee.

Jeff shared his office with Gary. It was a large room with a small kitchenette tucked behind bi-fold doors at the back of the room. A small refrigerator fit snuggly under the countertop, with a coffee maker and toaster on top. File cabinets lined the remaining wall. Behind Jeff a large window looked out into the service area of the building, while Gary had a window with a view of the showroom. There was no doubt that Gary's skill was in the auto sales. Jeff was training with Gary to learn his technique, but in the meantime, Jeff was in charge of the accounting.

Outside the door to the office, there were two counters. The first one was for sales transactions, and the second one was for service transactions. Gary and Jeff were fortunate to have kept two top-notch managers for these areas of the business, along with some part time people to help with some of the paperwork.

"Well, at least part of your search is behind you. New York, huh? Whereabouts is this place? Is it close to New York City?" Gary was curious.

"I haven't looked it up at all. There's an atlas on top the file cabinet." Jeff walked to the file cabinet to retrieve the atlas and brought it back to a table situated between their two desks. He flipped the pages to the map of New York State, checked the list of cities for Wahlberg and found the coordinates. From the mileage scale on the map, he and Gary decided it must be about an hour drive from New York.

"Well, I have a proposition for you," Gary said. "There is a car dealership meeting in New York City on Thursday. I had planned to attend, but my kids and grandkids have some important activities this week. If you could go in my place, you could make a run out to Wahlberg on Friday to see what you can find there. What do you think?"

Jeff blinked his eyes in wonder at Gary. "You mean attend the meeting instead of you? I really appreciate the vote of confidence, but I don't want you to do this just to help me out with my obsession!"

"No, just think of it as a coincidence of opportunity. It will really work out better for me this way. I'll see if I can get you on the flight I was going to take. Then I'll contact the organizers to get your name put in place of mine. It will be a good learning experience for you as well. Can you make the trip on this short notice?" Gary was pleased with the plan.

"Sure. No problem. I just need to be back on Friday night to go to Chatsworth on Saturday."

"Then we are all set. You can plan on going out on Wednesday night, and back on Friday night. Let's hope Friday is a good day to be in Wahlberg, New York."

Jeff was speechless. How could this work out so well for him? He needed to see if he could track down where Annie used to work, and then see if he could find Laurie, who Carrie indicated as Annie's friend in Wahlberg. In the meantime, he had to get some work done. He had been out of the office on Friday and Monday, now was leaving again on Wednesday night.

"Your flight is all set," said Gary, as he hung up the phone. "You can take my hotel reservation, as I was planning to stay on Thursday night also."

"Thanks, Gary. This means a lot to me."

Jeff worked late on Tuesday night to tie up some loose ends and lay out his day for Wednesday. Back at his apartment, he heated up a microwave dinner and flipped open a beer from the fridge. Molly sat beside him, a consistent beggar for table scraps. He would leave Molly with the vet for this short trip. She was due for a check up anyway. It occurred to him to call his mom and dad to tell them where he was going, but something stopped him. He decided to wait to talk to them when he returned. He thought of Carol. She would be off work by now and probably at home. He dialed her number.

"Hello?" the voice asked on the other end of the phone. It didn't sound like Carol's voice.

"Hello, is Carol there?"

"Yes, just a moment. Who should I say is calling?"

"Jeff Lipton."

"Well, hello, Jeff. I'm Carol's mom. You must be the nice young man Carol has been telling me about. I'll get her for you."

Carol came to the phone. "Hi, Jeff. How are things going?"

"It's good to hear your voice again, Carol." Jeff's pulse had quickened, and he smiled as he thought of her dressed in jeans and a sweatshirt with her hair pulled back. "Everything is going well. I talked to Annie's old college roommate the other night, and found out that Annie had lived in New York. Then on Tuesday, my boss asked me to go to New York City for a conference, and I'll have an extra day to go to the city where she lived, and apparently also died. It's been going kind of fast."

"I have some good news," Carol said. "My mom has been getting chemo treatments for cancer, and it looks like we have it in remission. Her tests today were really good, so we are relieved. Isn't that great?"

Jeff felt suddenly embarrassed. "Carol, I'm so sorry that I didn't ask more about why you were at home with your mom. I have no excuse for being so wrapped up in my own world. That is really great news!"

"It's okay. We don't talk about it too much to other folks. Mom wanted to beat it on her own and didn't want too much sympathy. She's been working when she can, and I've been here to help her through the rough times after the treatments. We are going to beat this together." Carol was enthusiastic.

"I was wondering if you had any plans for Saturday night." Jeff hoped she was free.

"Let's see, let me look at my social calendar. No, it looks like I have Saturday night open. What's up?" She was teasing.

"I'm going to Chatsworth to see Don and Sophie, so I thought I'd come by Green Meadow to see you later on in the afternoon, if that sounds good to you." There was something about Carol that made Jeff feel light-hearted.

"I'll tell you what. Why don't you call me here at the house when you are finished with Don and Sophie to let me know about what time I can expect you. We can get a bite to eat, and there is a movie I want to see, if you don't mind. It has both action and romance, so it's not a chick flick." Carol laughed at her own comment.

"That would be perfect. I'll see you on Saturday." Jeff hung up the phone and told Molly that she would have to meet Carol, as she would love her, and Carol would love Molly as well.

After dropping Molly off at the vet's on Wednesday afternoon, Jeff drove to the small airport at the edge of town and got on the flight to New York. The flight was uneventful and arrived on time. He rented a car and got directions to the hotel. After a short drive he was settled into his room at the Marriott. The convention was right there at the hotel, with registration at 7 AM. Jeff left a wake-up call, and was asleep almost when his head hit the pillow, the television still playing.

The convention was interesting. Jeff made notes of ideas for promotions to take back to the office. He met some other dealers from Iowa, and they exchanged cards with promises to get in touch. In the afternoon, there were breakout sessions on various aspects of the dealership business. Jeff attended the accounting one, and one on improving service delivery. The meeting adjourned at 5:00 with just enough time to change into better clothes for a dinner meeting. Everyone enjoyed cocktails until dinner was actually served, and it seemed to Jeff as though the day had flown by. He had learned so much about the inner workings of other dealerships, and had a few ideas of how to change some things back in Aubrey, with Gary's blessing, of course.

Jeff stopped at the concierge desk before going back up to his room. The attendant provided him with instructions for getting out of the city and onto the highway to Wahlberg. He recommended that Jeff check out of the hotel before leaving, so he could just drive straight back to the airport to catch his flight on Friday night, instead of first stopping at the hotel.

Jeff returned to his room feeling exhausted from the long day. He clicked on the TV to check on the weather for Friday, and found it to be clear skies and cold in New York. He laid out his clothes for the next day and repacked the rest of his suitcase, so he could get on the road early in the morning to beat the city traffic.

As Jeff lay in bed he wondered about Marty's phone call to Annie. What could that have been about? Was there some connection between Marty and Annie's death? What had happened to Laurie, Annie's friend? Did they work together at the bank? There had been so many banks bought and sold in the past 30 years that Jeff didn't know where to start, but he would just have to follow his gut. If he couldn't find anything on this trip, he would return another time. And then on Saturday, he would be talking to Don. Jeff was energized by the mystery around Annie's death. In his heart he wanted to believe that Annie was a good person, and that she loved him. He hoped he would still feel that way after tomorrow. He clicked off the TV and lay watching the lights from the signs dance on his sheer curtains, until he finally drifted off to sleep.

Jeff got up early on Friday, escaping the rush hour city traffic. He had some entertaining talk radio to keep him company on the way to Wahlberg. The directions were fairly simple, and the town was just off the main highway about five miles. Jeff took the exit and stopped for a cup of coffee before driving the remaining distance into town.

When he got into the city limits, he had to wonder what had drawn Mark and Annie to this place. The town was remote and fairly small. Jeff drove by a large Readi-Mart Warehouse on his right, with new apartment buildings on his left. A sign on the corner directed him to the business district, and as he approached the business district, he noted that there were two banks across the street from each other. He pulled into a parking place in front of the one on his right, and noted that it was almost 9 AM, just in time for banks to open for business.

As Jeff walked into the main lobby of the bank, he noticed that there were several desks on the left side, with tellers in windows on the right. He looked for an employee who might have been at the bank 30 years ago, and spotted a lady in her late 50s at the last desk in the row. He walked toward her and waited for her to motion for him to sit down.

"I don't know if you can help me. I'm looking for a woman named Laurie, who was a friend of Annie Moss. They worked in a bank some 30 years ago. Do you know if this might be the bank where they worked?" Jeff felt like he sounded like a magpie trying to get all the questions out.

"I'm sorry, sir, but I don't know who you are looking for. You might check with our Human Resources department. You will find that office on the second floor." The woman obviously didn't want to deal with Jeff, and almost shooed him away from her desk.

Dumb! Jeff wondered why he hadn't thought of the Human Resources department. He took the elevator up to the second floor, and looked for the sign pointing him in the right direction.

"Do you need an application?" the girl behind the desk asked him as he walked into the office.

"No, actually I'm looking for a current or former employee. Do you think you could help me?"

"What's the name?"

"The name is Laurie, and she was a friend of another employee, Annie Moss. This was about 30 years ago."

"30 years ago? I've only been here for five years. Is Annie Moss still working here?" The girl seemed interested, but was clueless as to how to find information.

"Annie Moss would have left about then. I don't know about Laurie, and I only have a first name. I thought maybe someone might remember them." Jeff sounded desperate.

"I've been here about 35 years, and I don't remember anyone by that name," a voice came from an office behind the girl's desk. A stout lady emerged from the office doorway to take a look at Jeff. "I don't think you will find them here." There was finality about her comment.

"Thanks anyway. I'll check with other banks here in town. Can you tell me where the other banks are located, other than the one directly across the street?"

"There's First National across the street and Citizen's down the street on your right. There's a new bank on the edge of town, but that wouldn't be the one you are looking for." The girl was trying to be helpful.

Jeff turned and walked back through the doorway to the office, took the elevator down to the first floor, and walked across the street to First National. This time, he looked immediately for directions to the Human Resources department.

"Do you need an application?" the young woman behind the counter asked. Jeff thought it sounded like a repeat performance from the first bank.

"No, I'm looking for a current or possibly former employee named Laurie. I don't have a last name. She was a friend to Annie Moss, who worked here until about 30 years ago." Jeff realized how impossible his information seemed.

"Annie Moss? I knew Annie Moss." A second person in the office turned and got up out of her chair. "She worked in check processing for quite a while, and was eventually in charge of that department. The Laurie you are looking for is Laurie Cameron. She and Annie were great friends, always had lunch together. I think they lived in the same apartment building."

Jeff was intrigued by her comments. "Did you know Annie very well?"

"No, just knew her because we worked here at the bank together." The woman in the suit walked over to a file cabinet in a remote corner of the room. She poked through several drawers and then leafed through file folders, until she finally pulled out a computer listing. "This is from 1973. See, here is Laurie Sue Cameron, and it lists her address. Then there is Annie Moss, same address, different apartment number. Let's see if I have a file on Laurie Cameron."

"Is it okay if I write down this address?" Jeff asked.

"I don't see any harm in it." She returned to the file cabinets and looked through a couple of additional drawers and files. "Here's Laurie Cameron. She left the bank in 1975. There's no forwarding address. It looks like Annie was terminated about the same time." She looked at Jeff, not sure if he was aware. "But, Annie was deceased."

"I know. It's okay. Thanks so much for helping me with this. I really appreciate it." Jeff was happy to have the address, but was disappointed about not finding Laurie Cameron. He had held out hope that she would still be working there, and could shed some light on Annie's life in Wahlberg. "Could you tell me where this address is here in the city?"

"That's not far from here." She gave him directions to find the apartment building. "If I'm not mistaken, it's still there."

Jeff left the Human Resources department of First National Bank, and walked back to his car. Following the directions, he made his way to the apartment building. Jeff sat outside the building for a while. There was a familiarity about the building. It seemed so small. He got out of his car and walked to the front door. Opening the front door, he instinctively knew that the stairs to the second floor were on the right, and there were mailboxes inside the door. He had been here before. He looked at the names on the mailboxes, and then turned to walk back to his car. He noticed that there was a little tavern on the corner, and thought he might find a sandwich there. It couldn't hurt to ask questions.

Jeff left his car parked at the apartment building, and walked to the tavern. He kept looking for signs of things he might recognize, as he was quite sure he had walked this street. The tavern was warm and welcoming, after the brisk walk from the apartments. He sat down at the bar and asked the bartender to bring him a beer and a menu. The menu was just one side of a single card, listing some sandwiches and soups. Jeff ordered a roast beef sandwich and a cup of the vegetable soup of the day. While he was waiting for the order, he asked the bartender, "Have you worked here long?"

"Name's Fred. Been here about 10 years, I suppose. Mr. Jenkins owns the bar. He bought it a long while back."

"Who's Mr. Jenkins?"

"Mr. Jenkins is a captain for the Wahlberg police department. He was a friend of the former owner. His name was Keith something. He got married and moved away, so Jack wanted to help him out. I work the day shift, and Jack tends bar in the evenings. He'll probably be by here for lunch." Fred dried out a couple of glasses as he talked to Jeff. "We have a pretty good lunch crowd."

Jeff listened with interest. Did he know Jack? There was no doubt he would have to wait around and see the owner of the bar. There might be a possibility that he would know Annie Moss and Laurie Cameron. He dropped a couple of quarters in the juke box and selected some music. His sandwich was good, as was the soup. He ordered a second beer and waited for Jack, still feeling an unusual sense of belonging.

Chapter 16
JACK AND MARTY

Jack left Annie's apartment and drove directly to the police station. He flipped on the light to his office, and retrieved his New York police directory. He quickly found the police station and the officers listed where Marty was being held. Further checking led him to the detective he wanted to be in touch with. Perhaps they could put their heads together on this one. But it might require Jack's going into the city to see Tom Wiseman in person.

Was Marty stable? If there was just a way to use him to get into the ring of drug dealers! Jack chewed on the end of the pencil in his hand, contemplating the call he would make to Detective Tom Wiseman. Finally, he dialed the number.

"Officer Reek speaking. May I help you?" was the response on the phone.

"This is Detective Jack Jenkins of the Wahlberg, New York police department. May I speak to Tom Wiseman, please?" Jack was hoping he was in.

"Just a moment, please. I'll check on Captain Wiseman for you." Jack heard the phone click to 'hold', and the music played in the background. If Wiseman thought he had a good collar, would he be at all interested in working with Jack?

The phone came back to life. "This is Tom Wiseman. How can I help you?"

"Thanks for talking to me, Tom. My name is Jack Jenkins and I'm a detective with the Wahlberg police department. A young lady here called me this evening to tell me she had received a phone call from her brother, Marty Ribold, who I understand you are holding there in your jail. Can you tell me the circumstances, and what state of mind Mr. Ribold is in?"

"Yeah, we have him here. He's in bad shape. Looks to me like he's been using too much of the drugs he is pushing. We caught him with some weed and some LSD, selling it to some college kids we had set up. Is there some particular reason you are involved in this?" Tom Wiseman was curious as to why an officer in another part of New York would be interested in his collar.

"It's kind of a long story. I'd like to make a trip there tomorrow to talk to you about Marty Ribold, and tell you about our ongoing investigation here. We believe there is a connection between some major suppliers here in Wahlberg and some of the college campuses. But I can tell you more about that if you will allow me to see you in person." Jack was pretty sure Tom would be receptive.

"Okay. Let me know when and how you will be arriving here, and I'll look forward to seeing you."

"That would be great. In the meantime, will you assure Mr. Ribold that you will be holding him there until later tomorrow before you charge him with anything? I think he is pretty shook up, and he's looking for his sister to help him out. I'll let her know I'll be coming into the city." Jack got some instructions on getting to the police station.

After hanging up the phone, Jack called Annie.

"Annie, I'm going into the City in the morning to visit with the Captain there of the police force. I'm not sure yet what we will work out, but I'll be in touch. In the meantime, just keep all this quiet until we know what we are going to do. You can tell Laurie, but make sure she doesn't breathe a word, okay? Be safe, Annie."

Jack didn't wait for Annie's response. He hung up the phone and started looking back through his files on Mark Moss. He had so little detail on what went down with Mark's beating. They had found drugs mixed in among the shipments on the truck, and they had found phone calls on the company phone bills. But when they traced them, they found only phony names and addresses. He still wasn't sure how much Annie knew of what was going on, but suspected that Mark had kept her in the dark for her own protection. Since Mark had decided to get out of the business, once he had learned of Annie's pregnancy, Jack had decided that Mark was probably a pretty decent guy. He had probably been sucked into the business when the money was easy and Mark needed the funding. He just hadn't realized how permanent the arrangement was assumed to be.

Annie. So beautiful. He wasn't sure just when she had become so important in his life, whether it was when he first questioned her at the police station, or when he first saw her that day in the park, long after Mark's death. She had always kept him at a distance, despite the fact that they spent time together in a group at the bar. A few dates had been fun, but Annie left no doubt that she intended for their relationship to be strictly platonic. He always hoped that if he gave her time, she might be more open to seeing him under different circumstances. Tonight he had held her briefly, but she had pulled away. He could remember the smell of her hair and the warmth of her body next to his. Jack shook his head and returned the file to its proper place in the cabinet.

The next morning, Jack drove to New York City. He had made some notes on possibilities for using Marty to get to the drug ring. In order to do that, he would have to get Tom Wiseman to release Marty to him, and allow him to bring him back to Wahlberg. Whew, no small assignment this one!

Tom was at the Police Station when Jack walked through the doors. He greeted Jack after he had introduced himself.

"I'm Tom Wiseman. Welcome to my town!" The officer was dressed in full uniform, complete with his gun and other portable equipment suspended from his belt. He moved his cigarette to his left hand and extended his right hand to Jack. The buttons on his uniform looked as though they might pop at any moment, as he placed his hands on his hips. He wore dark sunglasses, so Jack couldn't see his eyes. His smile pushed his chubby cheeks up to his sunglasses, and Jack couldn't help but smile in return. "Let's get going. How about lunch?"

"Lunch would be great. I'm starved, as I just grabbed a yogurt on my way out of town this morning."

"Now someone else might make some comment about eating a donut, but I'll pass on that opportunity." They walked out of the police station together. Tom motioned for Jack to get into the police car, and walked around to the driver's side. "I know a great place where we can get a bite, and visit some before we go into the jail."

Tom pulled into the traffic and drove to a restaurant a couple of miles away. He radioed into the dispatcher his location, and got out of the car. "Here we are. Now

this is on me, Jack. Well me, and the city of New York."
That smile again. Tom obviously enjoyed his own jokes.

The restaurant was a typical café with large windows
and a variety of tables and booths. Tom chose a booth
back in the far right corner, and asked the waitress to
bring them menus on his way through the tables.

They ordered their lunch. While they were waiting,
the two men talked briefly about their positions with the
police department and various challenges they both
faced. Tom had been Captain for about 10 years, and
had moved to the city from South Dakota about 10
years before that. He had some challenges with the
College, more in recent years than ever before. As in
many places, drug and alcohol use among the students
had increased substantially.

Jack knew they would not discuss Marty Ribold
until their food had been delivered, when there would
be no more chance of someone overhearing their
conversation. Once the food arrived, they assured the
waitress that they had everything they needed, and
Tom asked for some privacy.

"Okay, Jack. Let's hear what you have to say about
Marty Ribold." Tom picked up his soup spoon and
began to eat.

Jack filled Tom in on all the events leading up to
and then ending with Mark's beating death. There had
been some other collars since then, but they had not
had another opportunity to find as large a shipment

as they had found at the warehouse when Mark died. It was apparent that young people were getting drugs and using them, but their information sources had dried up. Jack believed that there was a connection between the drug rings in the city of New York and the small towns, and that they might be able to prove that with Marty Ribold.

"If we could get Marty to work with us, I think we could draw them out. My thought is to bring him to Wahlberg, and then to have him call his supplier to beg for mercy and another chance to make a drop or a major sale for them there. If the supplier works that out, we could be ready when Marty makes the drop." Jack waited for Tom to respond. Tom finished his soup and laid down his spoon.

"So you want to take my prisoner back to Wahlberg with you? How do your propose I take him off my books?"

"We can set this up as a sting operation. You and I would work together. Hell, you can even come to Wahlberg to work with me if you want. That way you would be in control of the prisoner if this doesn't work out, and you can bring him back. Look, Marty is just small potatoes. But if we could get some of the bigger fish, it would be great for both of us." Jack could see a gleam in Tom's eye.

"Wahlberg, eh? That might be interesting. But how will we get that little pipsqueak to agree to do this? Any ideas on that one?"

"I think the kid is really scared, from what Annie told me. So if we can offer him a way out of this if he helps us, then he might be willing. How much choice does he have at this point?" Jack gestured with his hands the hopelessness of Marty's current situation.

"When we finish up here, we'll go talk to the kid. The guys told me last night that he had the shakes from coming down from the drugs he's been using. We gave him some coffee, but I'm not sure that helped any. What is wrong with these kids? Wouldn't you think they could see what is happening to them?" Tom was obviously frustrated.

They talked more about the drug problems and other possibilities for getting to the major suppliers, as they finished their lunch. Tom finally motioned for the waitress to bring them the check. He gave her a nice tip and thanked her for giving them some private time. Tom was obviously well-liked in the area.

Marty was sitting in his cell, when an officer came to the door with a key, opened the door, and allowed two people into the cell. The first one was the captain of police, and was dressed in uniform. Captain Wiseman introduced the second man as Detective Jack Jenkins from the Wahlberg, New York Police Department. They sat on a bunk across from Marty, who was now alone in the cell.

Jack let Tom lead the conversation with Marty. "Jack here is a friend of your sister in Wahlberg. She called Jack after you contacted her last night. Marty, you are in a lot of trouble here, but we may have a way that you can help yourself by helping us."

"Wh...What do you want me to do?" Marty was very shaky, and Jack noted that he was perspiring profusely.

"We can spell out all the details later, but basically we want you to help us catch your supplier, and possibly other folks who might be involved in this drug ring you have gotten yourself into. Just hear me out, and I'll give you an idea of your role in all this." Tom proceeded to tell Marty of their plan to take him to Wahlberg and use him to contact not only his supplier, but possibly others who might get involved in a drug deal.

"Are you crazy? They will kill me!" Marty jumped up from the cot, and shouted at the two men.

"Sit down, son. Our plan is to be with you the entire time. You will be supported by police officers all around you if we can work this out. You will never be out of our sight. If you can do this, you can win your freedom and a chance to get yourself straightened out. You surely can't be happy with the way things are at the moment." Tom was firm with Marty.

"Marty, if you can help us with this, we can see to it that you get some help with rehab, and get away from all the trouble you have gotten yourself into. Your sister is very anxious for you to find your way out." Jack hoped that bringing Annie into the picture, Marty would be persuaded.

"I can't believe Annie cares about me. She ran away a long time ago, and neither my parents nor I have heard from her since. She had her own problems with drugs. Why would Annie care?" Marty was crying by this time.

"Annie does care," said Jack. "She called me right after you talked to her last night to see what we could do to help you. Annie is a very special woman, and she's counting on us to help you through all this. She can tell you all about what's been going on in her life if you come back to Wahlberg with me. What do you say, Marty?"

"Okay, I'll do as you say. I'm really hurting here. Can you get me anything for this?" Marty held out his hand, which was shaking violently.

"I'll see what I can do," said Tom. He called for the attending officer to take him and Jack back to the main station. He and Jack went into his office to do some paperwork for the transfer of the prisoner to Jack's precinct, as well as to line up support for the station while Tom went to Wahlberg. When he had a chance, Jack placed a call to Annie.

"Annie, Jack. I'm bringing Marty to Wahlberg with me. He has agreed to help us set up a sting to get to some of the people in this drug ring. I know it sounds a little dangerous, but we'll be with him all the time, if this even works out." Jack didn't know what to expect from Annie.

"Jack, that sounds far too dangerous. What kind of shape is he in?"

"He's a bit shaky and very nervous about the whole thing, but he really doesn't have a lot of options here. The captain of the police force here is coming back to Wahlberg with me to help with this operation. I can't tell you much more about it right now. I'm not sure it's wise to bring Marty to your apartment. Let's meet at the bar." Jack didn't want Annie involved any more than necessary, but he knew she would want to see Marty.

"Okay, Jack. I'll have Laurie come over to be with Jeff, and I'll meet you there. Jack, thanks so much for all you're doing."

"I wish I could say it was all for Marty and you, Annie, but you know how long we have all waited for a chance to get some of these guys, you included. We'll see you in a few hours." Jack hung up the phone as Tom came back into his office.

"We're all set. They're bringing the prisoner out in a few minutes. I told them I didn't think we needed handcuffs, since both of us will be with him all the time. Surely the two of us can handle that little guy!" Tom made a gesture with his fist.

Marty was led out into the main lobby, where Tom and Jack met him. The three of them got into Jack's police van and started their trip to Wahlberg.

Chapter 17
JEFF IN WAHLBERG

"Hey there, Captain!" the bartender greeted Jack as he came into the bar. Jeff noticed the man was out of uniform, dressed in jeans and wearing a leather jacket similar to his own. His hair was streaked with gray, giving him a distinguished appearance, and he walked with an air of confidence. He doffed his hat and coat, placed them on the coat tree by the door, and then walked over to the bar. He quickly ducked under the hinged counter to get behind the bar, and gave the bartender a playful fist to the stomach, barely touching him. They laughed as old friends.

"Have you had a good day, buddy?" Jack asked Fred, as he lifted the cash register tape to see the entries.

"Kind of quiet today, actually. By the way, there is someone here who has been waiting to talk to you."

Fred nodded his head toward Jeff. "I'll let you two introduce yourselves."

Jack looked at Jeff and walked toward him. He extended his hand and asked, "Jack Jenkins. Do I know you?" His brow furrowed in a frown, trying to remember if he had met the young man at another time.

"My name is Jeff Lipton, from Aubrey, Iowa."

Jack stood riveted to the floor behind the bar, still holding Jeff's hand in a firm grip, his heart racing. Could it be? He finally released Jeff's hand, and stood back, smoothing down his hair on the back of his head. "I don't believe it. How did you come to find me here?"

"I'm sorry," Jeff started. "But I think I've missed something here. Do you know me?"

Jack wasn't sure what to say to him. What did he know? "Okay, let's start over, Jeff. Can you tell me how you happened to be here at the bar, and why you were waiting for me?"

"It's a long story," Jeff said. "I have been looking for some information on a young woman and her friend who lived in this area about 30 years ago. The young woman's name was Annie Moss, and her friend's name was Laurie. I found the apartment building where they used to live, and just thought I'd stop here at this bar in hopes that someone might remember them. Annie Moss was my mother."

Jack walked to the end of the bar, lifted the counter doorway, and walked around to where Jeff was sitting.

"Jeff, I knew you when you were a little boy, and I knew your mother well. I can't believe you have come here to this place. It's been so many years!"

"You knew Annie?" Jeff was so excited, he almost knocked over his glass. "What can you tell me about her?"

"What have your parents told you, Jeff?" Jack suspected that Jeff's adoptive parents had not told him much about Annie or how they had come to adopt him. It put him in a very difficult position. Just how much could he tell this young man?

"They gave me my birth certificate from here in Wahlberg, along with some pictures of Annie and me, and a key. I have found her grave in Green Meadow, Iowa, and have located her father. In fact I will be seeing him tomorrow. I've also found out that her brother had contacted her shortly before her death, and that he was evidently mixed up with some drugs. Beyond that, everything is very sketchy. Her old college roommate gave me the name, Laurie, and I found the bank the two of them used to work for and their apartment building. It's just down the street from here. How did you know Annie?" Jeff's curiosity was peaked.

"Let's go over to a booth so we can talk. Do you have some time to spend with me? This is kind of a long and complicated story." Jack took Jeff's elbow to head him in the direction of a booth in the back of the room.

"I have a plane to catch later this afternoon, but am good until about 4 PM."

They sat down in the booth, and Fred brought Jack a sandwich. "Anything else I can get for you?" he asked Jeff.

"Just bring me a Diet Coke, if you would."

Jack smiled at Jeff. "Looks like you turned out pretty good! Must be that good Iowa air." He leaned over the table and took a bite of his sandwich, crossed his arms and leaned back in the booth.

"You said you knew that Annie's brother had called her shortly before her death. How did you find that out?" Jack wanted to get all the pieces in place.

"Annie's roommate Carrie told me that she had Annie's phone number, and that Marty had called to get the number. She said she had seen him a number of times and knew that he was into drugs. She also said that he sounded pretty anxious on the phone." Jeff wasn't sure why Jack had asked him about Marty.

"That's true. The night that he called Annie, she called me to tell me he was in trouble. He was being held at a police station in New York, on charges of possession and selling drugs. Jeff, do you know how your own father died?" Jack felt he was getting into some pretty treacherous waters with that question.

"No, I don't know anything about him. I know only that Annie ran away from college with him, and that her parents did not have contact with her after that."

"Well, let's start with Mark. It will help for you to know the background on Mark Moss, so you will understand the events that followed when Marty contacted Annie. Actually, that was when I first met Annie."

Jack told Jeff what he knew about Mark Moss, about his untimely death, and about Jack's interrogation of Annie as a detective on the case to find out more about Mark's involvement in drug trafficking.

"Let me just say, Jeff, many young people got caught up in the drug business back then. It was easy money, and the laws weren't clearly defined on how to deal with these folks. As I understand it, Mark was raised in an orphanage and had no trace of family. He got involved in the drugs as a young man in college, raising money to put himself through school. He brought Annie here to Wahlberg to take advantage of the setup at the warehouse. But when Mark found out that Annie was pregnant, they got married immediately, and soon after that, Mark had found a legitimate job. His attempt to get out of the drug business was what got him killed." Jack took another bite of his sandwich, and waited for Jeff's response.

"Do you know where Mark is buried?" Jeff asked.

"Yes, I can tell you where the cemetery is. It's a simple tombstone. We advised Annie not to attend the funeral, as we weren't sure if there would be people there looking to see if he had family in the area, and we didn't want her in danger. I didn't know at the time that she was pregnant with you."

"This is just too unbelievable. But go on with the phone call from Marty." Jeff was totally caught up in the mystery of his parents.

"Okay. I went to Annie's apartment and left there with the idea that I would get back to her with a plan to get Marty out of jail. Annie didn't want her parents to know Marty was in trouble. I contacted the captain of the police at the New York precinct, and together we devised a plan to possibly draw out the leaders of the drug ring that seemed to link Wahlberg with the City. I drove there the next day, and Captain Wiseman and I came back here with Marty. He had agreed to work with us to run a sting operation to catch his suppliers. The poor kid was trembling with withdrawal, and scared to death. We got back here late in the evening, and I had made arrangements with Annie to meet her here at the bar. Would you excuse me for just a moment? I need to make a quick phone call."

Jack slid out of the booth and stood to cross the room to the hallway, where a phone was mounted on the wall next to the men's room. Jeff watched him walk away, and then turned his gaze to the windows of the bar. He wondered if the streets still looked the same as when Annie would sit in here with her friends. A school bus drove by with it's cargo of youngsters. A taxi made a turn at the corner, after picking up a fare from the bar. A steady stream of pedestrians walked past the window. Jeff looked up as Jack returned to the booth.

"Now, where was I?"

Chapter 18
MARTY AND THE SETUP

"Marty, it's so good to see you. You are all grown up!" Annie opened her arms to hug her younger brother.

"Hi, sis. I'm so sorry to get you involved in all this." Marty was near tears again, his emotions totally out of control. He hugged Annie, holding her as though he might drown if he let go.

She broke the embrace, and placed her hands on his shoulders. "Don't you worry about what I think. I'm glad I could help. Are you okay with all of this?"

"I don't think I have a choice. I'm a wreck. Jack is going to take me to his place tonight so I can get a good night's sleep. Then tomorrow, I'll call my supplier and try to get this all set up. Annie, I'm so scared."

Annie could see that his physical and emotional condition were really shaky. Tears welled up in her eyes as she looked at him, holding his hands in reassurance.

Jack ordered a bowl of soup for Marty, along with a glass of milk.

"Marty, let's see if you can hold down some food. I know you haven't eaten in a while. When we get back to my apartment, we'll get you a shower and a comfortable bed, so you can get a good night's rest. Sound good, man?" Jack was trying to be reassuring.

Jack introduced Captain Wiseman to Annie. They talked very briefly about their plans, as Jack didn't want Annie to have all the details. Marty sipped a few spoons of soup and ate the crackers. He drank the milk hungrily, wiping away the milk mustache when he finished.

"Can we meet here again tomorrow?" Annie asked Jack. "I'd like to see if he's doing better tomorrow." She stroked Marty's arm. "I could meet you here on my lunch hour."

"I think that would be fine. We'll come by here again tomorrow for lunch, and you can meet with us then. In the meantime, I need to get Marty to my place for some R & R." Jack stood up to indicate the end of their conversation at the table. "Annie, everything's going to be okay." Jack took Annie's hand and squeezed it lightly, as he caught her eye.

"Jack, thanks for everything. I'll see you tomorrow. Good night, Captain Wiseman." Annie turned and left through the front door of the bar. She reached into the collar of her jacket and flipped her long hair out to release it.

"Well, I guess it's pretty clear why you have gotten involved with this situation!" Captain Wiseman had a gleam in his eye, as he grinned at Jack. "Wow!"

Jack paid the tab and escorted Marty out to the car. He dropped Tom off at a motel near his apartment, and took Marty back with him. While Marty was getting a shower, he found some of his own pajamas, as well as some clothes for the next day for Marty to wear.

Marty lay awake for a long time before finally falling asleep from exhaustion. He watched the light patterns as the lights of the city reflected on the ceiling of the bedroom. The clock ticked loudly on the nightstand, as though to issue some sort of warning of the passing of time. His brief moments of sleep were filled with nightmares of possible outcomes of his proposed encounter with the drug suppliers, none of them pleasant. He tossed and turned, and even cried out in his sleep early in the morning, waking Jack in the next room. Jack checked in on him, and then sat in the recliner staring off into the darkness, as he contemplated the day.

Early the next morning, Marty heard Jack in the kitchen, and in a few minutes, he could smell the fresh coffee brewing. He felt tired and drawn, and his hands were still shaking.

"Good morning! Did you sleep at all?" Jack asked Marty.

"Not much. Too nervous. I'm not sure what you want me to do." Marty started to get out of the bed. His clothes were laid out for him on a chair near the bathroom door.

"Let's get a bite to eat, and then we will talk about our next step. Some coffee will help wake you up," Jack said.

Marty grabbed the clothes and went into the bathroom, turning on the shower. Jack heard the shower running, and went back to the kitchen to scramble some eggs and make some toast. He checked to see that he had enough eggs, then laid out some bacon in the skillet and turned on the burner. By the time the bacon was finished frying, Marty had joined him in the kitchen, still looking pale and gaunt and very nervous. Jack poured him some coffee.

"Cream and sugar?" he asked.

"No. Just black, thanks." Marty accepted the cup of coffee from Jack and settled down into a chair by the table. "The bacon smells good." Marty took a sip of the coffee.

"This is just about the extent of my cooking, except for the grill outside. I'm always on the go, so don't have much time for learning to cook." Jack watched Marty as he held the cup precariously. His hair was still wet from the shower and was combed back from his face.

Jack could see a resemblance to Annie, especially in his eyes. Marty was slender, but appeared to have worked out some, given the muscle tone in his arms.

"Are you seeing my sister?" Marty asked, watching as Jack cracked eggs into a bowl. The bacon was laid out on a paper towel, draining.

"We are just good friends. Annie called me because she thought I might be able to help you." Jack didn't look at Marty, but was whisking the eggs and milk and pouring them into the pan. "We've gone out a few times, but just to a movie or concert. Why do you ask?"

"Just curious. I don't know much about Annie. She left home to go to college, then left college evidently to come here to New York with that guy Mark. She and my mom were not on the best of terms, and Annie chose not to stay in touch. Mom was really bummed out about it at the time. I think she just decided to accept Annie being gone, and just hoped that one day she would come home." Marty shrugged, indicating his passive participation in their home life.

"And what about you? How did you get yourself into this mess, Marty?" Jack stirred the eggs in the skillet as they cooked, finally dumping portions onto two plates for himself and Marty. He carried them to the table, and then also grabbed the bacon. The toast popped up in the toaster, and he spread some butter on it before taking a slice for himself and handing one to Marty.

"It's kind of a long story. I started using in high school, then got connected with this guy who said I could get my own stuff free, if I'd help him distribute. He said he would pay me by the amount I delivered. I collected the money, and then he would get me a percentage. It was all done by an envelope in a lock box, so I never saw the guy again. Our contact was always by phone. The money really came in handy at college. I just finished school, and was going to get out of the business when I got busted. Now, here I am with you." Marty ate his breakfast hungrily. He slathered some jelly on his toast and ate that as well. They ate silently for a few moments.

"Marty, when we finish with breakfast, I want you to call your supplier. You need to tell him that you screwed up and got caught, that you have lost the money and the drugs, and that you are in Wahlberg, New York. Then I want you to ask him if you can make it up to him by making a delivery here in Wahlberg. We strongly suspect that there is a connection between the City college campuses and the distribution here in Wahlberg." Jack finished his breakfast, and wiped his mouth with a napkin.

"I can't do that!" Marty was immediately seized with fear. "They will kill me!" He threw his napkin onto the table.

"I know you are afraid, Marty, but we need to get an opportunity to catch these guys. You will not be alone.

We will be constantly monitoring your every move, and there will be officers stationed all around you. We just need to draw them out into the open." Jack talked with confidence and emphasized the importance of Marty's participation.

Marty stood and started pacing the floor. "I know what happened to Annie's husband, Mark. I'm not stupid! I might as well just put a noose around my neck!" He glared at Jack, and then looked away. Tears were forming in his eyes. "You want me to just be your guinea pig!"

Jack grabbed his arm. "Sit down, Marty. This is your get-out-of-jail-free card. You either do this with us, or you go back with Captain Wiseman and face the music. It won't be an easy out, that's for sure." Jack was firm and losing patience.

Marty sat in the chair and looked at Jack. Jack's jaw was set, and the rippling muscles indicated that he was gritting his teeth. He loosened Jack's grip on his arm and pushed him away.

Jack could see that the man was panicked.

"Look, Marty. Like I said, we will be with you all the time. I'll write out what you need to say when you make the phone call. You can rehearse it until you feel comfortable. Everything will work out fine." Jack took Marty's breakfast plate and his own and carried them to the sink.

"I'll do what I have to do to get out of the rap. I'll be back in a minute." Marty pushed back the chair, and stood up to walk back to the bedroom. There he put on some socks and shoes, and buttoned his shirt. He stopped in the bathroom to finish combing his hair and used the extra toothbrush Jack had left out for him. He looked in the mirror, and again fought back tears. His hands were still shaking, and he noted the wild look in his eyes.

Jack placed the dishes in the dishwasher and wiped up the kitchen. Then he sat down at the table to write out the script for Marty to use to call his supplier. It had to sound sincere, and it wouldn't matter if Marty sounded frightened on the phone. The supplier would expect him to be scared. The important thing would be that he would take the bait.

Marty came back into the kitchen and read through the script Jack had prepared. He made a couple of suggestions for changes, and then read it aloud to Jack. After several times through the script, Marty placed the call.

"This is Marty. I've really screwed up, and I'm out on bail. My sister lives in Wahlberg, New York, and I've been released to her for the time being. The delivery and the money were confiscated by the police. I'm really sorry. Is there anything I can do to make it up to you?" Marty's voice was shaky on the phone, but he managed to sound sincere.

Marty held the phone so Jack could hear the response. "You really did screw things up. You've lost us a ton of money! Can you get away from your sister?"

"Yeah. She works, so she's gone during the day, and doesn't get home until after 6." Jack had anticipated the question.

"I'm going to give you a chance to make this up. We need to move some product. You'll need to get a back pack, and then go to the car repair shop on the corner of Locust and 7th street around 4 P.M. Identify yourself as Marty to the owner, Ralph. Ralph will take you to a room where you will load up the product in the back pack. Take the bus from there to the park at the end of Adams Street. There is a pavilion there that is deserted in the late afternoon. You should be there around 5. Leave the backpack in the trash bin on the east side of the pavilion, and walk away. We'll take care of it from there. And Marty, don't screw this up this time! Got it?"

"Yes, I've got it. And thanks for giving me another chance. I'll be there." Marty hung up the phone, ashen from the exchange.

"You did it! Good job!" Jack clapped his hands in excitement. The doorbell rang, and Jack opened it to Captain Wiseman. "We made the call, and the pick up and drop is set up. I knew there was a connection to here in Wahlberg!"

Captain Wiseman looked at Marty. "You okay, kid?" he asked, noting Marty's physical appearance and apparent state of mind.

"No. Not really. This is just a set up to do away with me, I know it."

"Well, we just won't let that happen. Jack here has his police force set up to be right there with you all the time. We'll be watching and ready for action." Wiseman looked at Jack for reinforcement.

"The instructions are for Marty to take a backpack into a room at the car repair shop, so he will be out of our sight for a few minutes at that time. But my guess is that if there are going to be any other people involved it will be at the drop, not at the pick up point. What do you think?" Jack looked at Wiseman.

"I'd say you are right. Is the delivery far from the pick up point?"

"It's across town at a park at the end of Adams Street. That's where we will need the most reinforcement. We need to talk about our strategy. Let's take a drive down by the park and the pavilion and lay out our plans. Marty can also get a chance to see where we want him to be after he makes the drop. By then, it will be time for lunch, and I promised your sister we would meet her at noon at the bar." Jack grabbed his weapon and strapped it on, then motioned for Wiseman and Marty to follow him out of the apartment.

They drove out Adams Street, into the park, and located the pavilion and the trash can where Marty was to make the drop with his backpack. The two officers agreed that any takedown would happen after Marty deposited the backpack. The suppliers wouldn't take any chances on the safety of the drugs. Jack looked over the park for possible areas to place his officers, and felt they could set up the trap effectively. He made some notes to take back to the police station to brief his men. They also drove past the car repair shop to see if there was a parking spot where they could place an unmarked car to watch Marty going in and coming out. Jack planned to have a wire on Marty as well as a bullet-proof vest under his down jacket for his safety.

At almost noon, they arrived at the bar, and walked in together to meet Annie. She came in a few minutes behind them, and joined them at a table. They all ordered the barbecue sandwich special for the day. Jack briefed Annie on the progress they had made.

"Marty, are you doing okay with all of this?" she asked her brother.

Marty looked at her, his eyes moist with tears. "I'm so scared, Annie. I had nightmares last night about this whole thing, and I don't feel any better about it today." He took her hand, his own hand trembling.

"Jack, he is in no condition to pull this off today. You can't send him out there in this condition!" Annie looked at Jack with fire in her eyes.

"Annie, we don't have any choice. We've got this whole thing set up, and there is no turning back now."

"Then I'm going instead of him." She crossed her arms and sat back in her chair.

"What? You are not! Marty has been briefed and is ready to do this!" Jack was determined.

"Well, then you will have to brief me instead. I'll not allow you to send my brother into this in his condition. Look at him. He can't even think straight. If you are going to be right there during this whole thing, then you can watch over me just as well as you can watch over Marty."

"Annie, you can't do this," Marty said. "I'll be okay, and it will be over before you know it."

Annie looked into his eyes. "Look, little brother. I'm not about to lose you like I did Mark. You and I are close enough to the same build that I can pull this off. I'll be perfectly safe. And you'll be a free man to go back and get your life together."

Jack looked at Wiseman. "Annie may have a point about Marty's state of mind," he said. "What do you think?"

"It's a risk, no matter how you cut it, Jack. If you have her wired and wearing a vest, you'll cut the risk. She's pretty determined." Wiseman grinned at Annie. "I like a girl with spunk!"

Annie ignored him. "Then it's settled. I'll call in sick to work this afternoon, and you can bring me up to speed. What time is this thing supposed to go down?"

Jack smiled at her enthusiasm and ran a hand through his hair in frustration. "Annie, you are impossible. Are you sure you want to do this?"

"I've never been more certain of anything in my life. It will be my chance to avenge Mark's death. You just be ready to catch these guys when it's all said and done, got it?" Annie winked at Jack. The sandwiches were delivered to their table, and they talked about the plans for the operation.

Chapter 19

ANNIE: THE SHOWDOWN

Annie was excited about her role as a police operative. She called the bank from Jack's place to tell them she had something come up. Then she called Laurie's line.

"You won't believe it! I'm helping Jack with this drug thing. Marty's in an awful state, and it just makes sense for me to do this. Would you be a dear and pick Jeff up from day care? I'll be in touch as soon as I'm free. Should be a little after 6." Annie could hardly control her excitement.

"You're what?! Are you crazy?" Laurie exclaimed. "Annie this sounds really dangerous!"

"Jack and the entire police force are going to be right there with me. I'll be fine. Give Jeff a big kiss for me! And Laurie, if something should happen to me, take care of him for me, will you?" Annie hung up the phone before Laurie could say another word.

Annie walked into Jack's kitchen. Jack had put on a tea kettle for some hot water for tea, and had set out mugs and teabags on the table. Marty was in the living room, watching TV and occasionally dozing off to sleep. The tea kettle began to whistle on the stove.

"Annie, are you sure about this? I know you are determined, but I'm concerned about what you are getting yourself into. Things could go wrong, you know." Jack poured the hot water into their mugs, leaving Marty's empty for the time being.

Annie smiled at him. "I know you are concerned, but I'm quite sure I can pull this off. Certainly I can do a better job than Marty. And there may not be anything at all to be concerned about. You will be able to catch the guy at the service station and whoever picks up the delivery at the park, and that may be all there is to it. Hopefully, one of them will be able to finger a bigger catch for you." Annie selected a tea from the basket of tea bags and dipped it in the hot water. Then she added a teaspoon of sugar and stirred it in, all the time watching Jack.

"Okay. So here's how it's going to go." Jack proceeded to tell Annie about the pick up in the back pack, the trip by bus to the park, and the drop at the pavilion. He explained where officers would be stationed at each location, emphasizing that he and Captain Wiseman would both be at the park watching the pavilion. "Annie, there were at least two involved in

Mark's beating death. Since Marty has told his supplier that he has screwed up and lost money and drugs, this may be a set up to draw Marty out for the same treatment. It could be dangerous."

Annie stood up and walked to the living room doorway to check on Marty. Seeing that he was sleeping, she walked back to the table. "Jack, Marty doesn't have the ability to think fast enough to work through this with you. I don't see that I have a choice. You'll be right there to intercept anyone who might be waiting for me at the pavilion. You may have already identified them by the time I get there. As I see it, we can't fail. And you will finally be able to put this behind you." Annie leaned over and kissed Jack on the forehead, then sat back down at the table.

"If anything happened to you, I couldn't forgive myself, Annie. You know how much I care for you, don't you?" Jack looked into her eyes.

Annie was pensive for a moment. She reached across the table to put her hand over Jack's. "Yes, I do. Maybe one day things will work out for us. Who knows? Jeff is my life right now, and I choose to devote all my energy to raising him. I really appreciate all you have done for me and for Marty." She drew her hand back to her mug.

The doorbell rang, and Captain Wiseman was at the door. "Are we ready?" he asked, as he came into the kitchen, stopping only momentarily to check on

Marty. "What are we going to do about the kid while we are out?" He looked at Jack for a solution.

"We'll drop him off at the police station to stay with an officer there until I get back. Sound okay?" Jack glanced at Annie. "Annie is all set."

The three of them walked into the living room, and Annie shook Marty to wake him. Then they left for the police station to leave Marty. The plan was to allow Annie to take the bus to the car repair shop, and then get back on the bus to go to the park. She had her hair tucked up under a cap, and wore no makeup. She also wore boys' jeans, a shirt that hid a bullet proof vest, and a jacket. Jack and Captain Wiseman agreed that no one would guess she was a woman. Annie got on the bus from the police station, and started on her quest.

She arrived at the car repair shop right at the appointed time with her backpack, and walked into the station. Everything in the place looked grimy and dingy. The floor was caked with oil and dirt, and the counter and cash register were dusty and stained with grease. A heavy set woman Annie estimated to be in her 50s stood up and came to the counter as Annie entered the room. She wore tight knit pants and a blouse that was hiked up to her waste in the back, emphasizing her large anatomy.

"I'm looking for Ralph." Annie was careful to use a lower tone in her voice and to not look directly at the woman behind the counter.

"Just a minute. I'll get him for you. What's your name?"

"Name's Marty. Ralph is expecting me."

Annie watched the woman waddle through a door behind the counter and out into the repair shop area. She stopped by a car in the shop, and appeared to be talking to the floor, pointing back at the counter, where Annie was waiting. She heard the sound of the wheels of the scooter on the concrete, and saw a tall, thin man stand up, wiping his hands with a shop rag. He tucked the rag into his hip pocket, and walked toward the door.

"Come with me," he said to Annie.

Annie felt her heart racing, as she walked through the door and followed Ralph. They walked down a narrow hallway and into a stock room, which was filled with racks of various auto parts and accessories. The room smelled of oil and grease mixed with dirt and dust. Ralph continued on between the shelving to a small door in the back of the room. Annie thought Ralph could hear the beating of her heart by now, as she walked through the door, not knowing what to expect on the other side. Ralph reached up, and took down a package from the top shelf, wrapped in plain brown paper.

"Open up your backpack, and we'll get this into it." Ralph motioned for her to take off her backpack.

"Oh, sure," said Annie, removing the backpack.

Ralph placed the package in the backpack, and zipped it up. Annie put the backpack on, struggling momentarily with the left strap. Ralph turned back to the door, and continued on back to the main service area with Annie following close behind. She looked from side to side as they walked back between the shelves, half expecting someone to jump out and grab her at any moment. Once back in the service area, Ralph lay back down on the scooter, as though there was no big concern, and pushed himself under the service car. He left Annie to go on her way without another word.

Annie walked out the front door and continued on to the bus stop. She noted that about twenty minutes had passed. If the bus made several stops on the way to the park, she should be at the pavilion right on time. She stood at the bus stop, looking around for any indication of Jack's people.

Across the street a man was sitting on a bench reading a paper. He seemed to be totally oblivious of Annie. A woman was pushing a stroller down the sidewalk toward her, stopping occasionally to look in the windows of the stores as she passed. Several people were waiting with Annie to get on the bus when it arrived. As far as Annie could see, none of them was recognizable as a police officer, so she had no idea if someone was watching over her. A chill ran through her to think she might be on her own.

The bus arrived, and Annie boarded with the others who were waiting. The park was the last stop at the end of Adams Street, and Annie would be the last one out. She wondered if someone would get off with her. The pavilion was a pretty good walk through the park. Jack's people couldn't risk being seen following her to the pavilion.

It seemed like an eternity to Annie as the bus made stop after stop, letting people off and picking people up. Annie looked out the window, lost in thought. Mark. Jeff. What would life have been if Mark had lived? He would have been a wonderful father to Jeff. He was so excited about the pregnancy. Annie smiled as she thought about the day she told him. What would Marty do now that he was going to get a new chance to get his life straightened out? What about her parents? A strange feeling came over Annie as she thought about her parents. It had been nearly six years since she had seen them or talked to them. Her life was totally caught up in Jeff, work, and her friends. She just couldn't imagine what their reaction would be to news of Jeff. It had been so long now. But maybe she could contact them. She thought back to those days in high school and college and how she had behaved toward her mother. Would Jeff treat her like that some day? Annie shuddered at the thought, suddenly jolted by the movement of the bus.

The bus hissed to a stop at the park. "Last stop for this line!" the bus driver announced. Annie picked up her backpack, which she had laid at her feet, and strapped it on as she made her way to the front of the bus. One lady got off the bus with her, turning to walk toward the lake. Annie spotted the pavilion and headed that direction.

The day was overcast, but still unseasonably warm. Annie was really uncomfortable with the vest, the shirt, and the jacket, plus the backpack on her back. She followed the walking path toward the pavilion, looking around for any sign of Jack. The pavilion was deserted. She started up the stairs to the deck around the pavilion, where the trash can was located. Her heart was racing again, and perspiration was forming on her forehead. She couldn't take off the hat and expose her long hair, so she wiped her brow with the sleeve of her jacket. It was so quiet, that she could hear her own heavy breathing as she climbed the stairs. A twig snapped to her right, and she looked in time to see a small dog run off into the woods.

Annie took off the backpack when she arrived at the trash can. She took out the package that she and Ralph had placed there, and put it into the container. Just as she was zipping up the backpack, a man emerged from a door of the pavilion, not five feet from her. She froze in fear, as he started walking toward her. He walked with a swagger and did not say a word. After just a few steps he was stopped in his tracks.

"Hold it right there!" Jack's voice broke the silence. The man quickly ducked back into the doorway. "Annie, get the hell out of there! Run!"

Annie grabbed the backpack and ran back across the deck and down the stairs. Her legs felt like gelatin, so she clung to the railing. She started running toward Jack, when she saw out of the corner of her eye a man emerging from the shadows of the pavilion and aiming a gun at Jack.

"Jack, watch out!" Annie looked back at Jack to warn him, but put herself in the line of fire. Gunshots. A burning pain. Annie grabbed her neck and fell to the ground.

"Annie!" Jack was at her side in an instant, and immediately noticed that she had been hit. Blood was spurting from her neck. "God! You have been shot!" Jack put his finger on the wound in her neck. He lifted her head gently to see if the bullet had emerged on the other side, and found another wound. He applied pressure to both wounds. "Get an ambulance. Annie's been shot!"

The scene was total chaos. Officers were running after the shooter, and others were breaking down the door to the pavilion. Wiseman placed the call to 911 to get the ambulance there, telling them of the situation. The shooter was apprehended and shoved to the ground face down. Other officers emerged from the pavilion pushing a second man toward the squad cars in hand cuffs.

"Stay with me, Annie. You have to stay with me." Jack was white as a ghost, continuing to hold pressure on the wounds in Annie's neck. Annie had lost consciousness, and Jack knew this was serious.

The ambulance arrived and the EMT's quickly assessed the situation. They had Jack continue to hold pressure on the wounds as they loaded Annie into the ambulance, and then sped off to the hospital, only moments away.

As they wheeled Annie into the emergency room, there were doctors waiting for her arrival. The EMT's had called ahead to tell them of the gravity of the situation. "We'll take her immediately into surgery," the doctor told Jack. "We don't have much time. I suspect the bullet has hit an artery in her neck."

They wheeled Annie down the hall and into an elevator, and Jack walked to the desk. "Where can I go to wait for word on the surgery?" he asked the nurse at the desk. "I'm Detective Jack Jenkins of the Wahlberg Police Department."

"Well, Jenkins, you can go to the fourth floor. There is a waiting room there for surgical patients. If you just jot down your name for me, I'll get word to the surgical staff to find you there when she comes out of surgery. Can you give me the patient's name and information?"

"Sure. Her name is Annie Moss." He gave her the address and phone number and where she worked. Then he called Laurie.

"Laurie, there's been an accident, and Annie is in surgery. I'll tell you all about it, but knew you would want to be here. Better not bring Jeff. Can you leave him with someone there?" Jack's voice was shaking and panic-stricken.

"I'll be there in a flash," replied Laurie. "Jack, is she going to be okay?"

"I don't know yet. They took her right into surgery, and I have no idea how long it will be." Jack drew his hand down over his face. "I'll see you when you get here. I'll be in the fourth floor waiting room."

He placed the phone back into the cradle, and then picked it up again to call the station. "This is Jack Jenkins. I need to talk to Marty Ribold, the young man we brought by the station this afternoon." Jack waited as the officer at the desk got Marty to the phone.

"Hello?"

"Marty, there's been an accident, and Annie has been hurt. I'm at the hospital, and they have taken her into surgery. Is Wiseman back at the station yet?"

"Yes, he's right here. Is Annie going to be okay?"

"I don't know yet. Let me talk to Wiseman, and I'll have him bring you to the hospital."

Captain Wiseman took the phone from Marty. "How's Annie doing?"

"I don't know yet. They have her in surgery. I need for you to bring Marty to the hospital to the fourth floor waiting room. I don't know how long Annie will be in surgery, but the doctors were pretty grim. Can you do that for me? How did everything go?"

"We caught the two guys at the park, and there's a patrol car going to the car repair shop to pick up Ralph. We also have the package that was delivered to the pavilion. I'll be right there with Marty." Captain Wiseman hung up the phone and motioned for Marty to follow him to the squad car.

People arrived one by one at the waiting room. Laurie came in and gave Jack a hug. She was followed close behind by Keith from the bar. Captain Wiseman arrived with Marty, who was by now feeling total guilt for Annie's accident. He paced behind the row of chairs, chewing his fingernails and muffling an occasional sob. Keith held Laurie's hand as they drank coffee and waited for news from the surgery team. The room was tastefully decorated with drapes on the windows and comfortable chairs for those awaiting word on loved ones. A coffee urn with fresh coffee was set up in one corner of the room, surrounded by Styrofoam cups, sugar and sweetener packets, and a dispenser with cream. Outside the room, there were vending machines with snacks and cold drinks. Paintings of landscapes and gardens graced the walls. Two television sets were mounted near the ceiling in opposite corners, so that different programming could be selected. On a coffee table, dishes held a variety of mints and chocolates. Each family or group talked in hushed tones out of respect for others who were waiting. Clocks mounted on two walls, ticked away the seconds and minutes as time seemed to crawl by.

"Detective Jenkins, I have a call for you." A volunteer manned the desk where doctors could call to inform loved ones of the progress.

"Jenkins, this is Doctor Mason. We have the bleeding stopped for the moment, and we are repairing the damage. The bullet passed through, so we did not have to dislodge it from her neck. The injury is to the carotid artery, and the repair is very tedious. There are many things that could go wrong once we have completed the surgery, so we will be watching her very carefully. I'll call you again when we are taking her to the intensive care unit. She will be groggy for some time, but you may be able to go in to see her. It will be very important not to excite her."

"Thank you for letting me know, Doctor. I'll be here waiting for your call." Jack hung up the phone and turned to the others. "Annie is still in surgery. The bullet is out, and they have made repairs to her carotid artery. But her recovery is very tentative. The doctor said even when they get her out of surgery, she will be in intensive care, and they will be watching her very closely. But at least she is alive!"

"So do we wait here for now?" asked Laurie.

"You can wait as long as you want. He will call again when they are finished, and we can go in to see her. He just said not to excite her. She'll be groggy for some time." Jack hugged Laurie again. "You are such a good friend."

They all took chairs again, after filling coffee cups and getting sodas from the vending machines. And they waited. Keith and Laurie were having a private conversation in one corner of the room. Marty was pacing. Jack and Captain Wiseman talked in hushed tones about the operation and what may have gone wrong. They were also in some turmoil about how to handle Marty, with Annie in the hospital.

Finally the phone rang again on the waiting room desk. "Detective Jenkins, it's for you."

Jack walked quickly to the desk and took the phone. "This is Jack Jenkins."

"This is Doctor Mason again. We have taken the patient down to intensive care. She woke up in the waiting room, and is asking for you and for a Laurie. Is Laurie there with you?"

"Yes, she's right here with me. How do things look for Annie, Doctor?" Jack's voice reflected his concern for Annie.

"Well, it's not good. She will be in a very precarious situation for several days. And, as I told you before, there are many things that could go wrong. It will be important that we try to keep her as calm as possible to give the repairs time to heal. She will be very groggy. I've told her of the gravity of her situation, so she knows she should get any necessary affairs in order, preparing for the worst. You will be able to see her in the intensive care unit on the 3rd floor. I've left instructions for people to go in just one at a time. Good luck to you." The doctor hung up the phone.

Jack walked back to the others to relay the news. "Things are looking bleak at the moment. The repairs have been made, and Annie is in the intensive care unit. She woke up in recovery, but will be groggy. The doctor is only allowing one person at a time in to see her. We can all go to the third floor, and we'll check in there with the nurses' station. I'd suggest that Marty go in first. Everyone okay with that?"

The suggestion was accepted unanimously, and they all walked together to the elevator and down to the third floor. Marty went in first to see Annie.

When he walked into her room, he was shocked at all the electronic equipment, bottles, and tubes surrounding her bed. Annie looked pale and her hair was unkempt. Bandages were wrapped around her neck, and she lay very still.

"Annie?" Marty was almost afraid to see her open her eyes. He was filled with emotions of guilt, pity, and love for Annie.

Annie opened her eyes and talked in a hushed voice. "Hi, Marty. Thanks for coming in to see me. I want you to promise me that you will get yourself straightened out. Get back to New York so Mom and Dad won't know you were here. I'm going to ask that they be contacted, and you need to be out of here. I'll talk to Jack about what we will tell them about my injury. This is your chance, Marty. Don't screw it up, okay?"

"I won't. I promise. I love you, Annie. Thanks for everything you have done for me." Marty laid his head down on his sister's shoulder, tears streaming down his face. He lifted his head to see that Annie had closed her eyes again. He rubbed her arm gently, then turned and left the room.

"I got to talk to her," Marty said, as he came out to be with the others. "Be prepared for all the equipment they have hooked up to her."

Jack turned to Laurie. "Do you mind if I go in to see her briefly before you go?"

"Go ahead, Jack," said Laurie. "I'll wait here."

Marty sat down with Captain Wiseman, and Jack walked the short distance to Annie's room. He was gripped with anger and remorse at seeing her lying in the bed, her every vital sign being monitored by the equipment. She had been so insistent on taking Marty's place, and now here she was lying so close to death. He had been so stupid to allow this to happen. They had prepared for guns, but they were only expecting that the thugs would want to physically attack Marty. If Annie died, how would he ever live with himself?

"Annie, it's Jack," he whispered. Annie opened her eyes to look at him.

"Hi, Jack. I'm so sorry this got so messed up. That guy came out of nowhere, and he was aiming his gun at you." Annie spoke barely above a whisper.

"Don't worry. Do you know you helped to capture the two at the pavilion as well as the middle man at the car repair shop? They are all in custody." Jack wanted her to know they had been successful in apprehending them. "You are quite a brave lady!" He smiled at Annie, giving her hand a squeeze.

She tightened her hold on his hand. "Jack, if I don't pull through this, don't blame yourself, okay? This was all my own doing, so it's all my own fault."

"Annie, I shouldn't have let you do it. We should have found a better way." Jack's eyes were moist with tears. Annie reached up and touched his face.

"You're a good man, Jack Jenkins. I want you to get Marty out of here and back to the City. When he is gone, I want you to contact my parents in Green Meadow, Iowa. I don't want them to know anything about Marty, so we have to decide what you are going to tell them about what happened to me. They also can't know about Jeff. I'll work that out with Laurie. She'll take care of Jeff for me. Can you do all this for me, Jack?" Annie's eyes were pleading.

"I'll do whatever you ask, Annie. But you are going to be fine. You just need your rest. I need to get out of here, and I'll send Laurie in to see you. I'll get Marty and Captain Wiseman on their way, and then come back. All you need to do is call on me, and I'll be here." Jack stood up and kissed her on the forehead. Then he laid her arm down at her side, pulled up the covers, and left the room.

"Tom, I need to get you and Marty back to New York. I trust that you will see that Marty gets back to his apartment, and I'd like to see you watching over him for a while. He'll be moving out soon to either go to his folks, into rehab, or on to a new job, right Marty?" Jack put his hand on Marty's shoulder.

"That's right. Annie made me promise. And thanks, Jack, for all you've done for me." Marty shook Jack's hand. The three of them left the intensive care unit together. Laurie went down the hall to Annie's room, leaving Keith to wait for her in the waiting area.

Chapter 20
JEFF

Jack leaned back in the booth and looked at Jeff. "That's pretty much how it all went down. As you know, Annie didn't make it. The doctors said that her blood pressure spiked and burst the stitches they had used in the repairs. Her folks did get here from Iowa before she died, and she got to see them. We got Marty back to the city, and as far as I know, they did not know of his role in the tragedy."

"But what about the adoption? Where is Laurie? What do you know about her involvement with Annie?" Jeff was anxious to get answers to those questions.

"Captain Jenkins, phone for you!" Fred called from behind the bar.

"Excuse me Jeff, but I'll have to take this call." Jack slid out of the booth and walked behind the bar to take the phone from Fred. He hung up the phone and walked by the booth. "Jeff, I have to run. It's been good to talk to you, and I hope you will come by again. Sorry I don't have all the answers for you. You might want to stop by to see your folks to let them know what you have found out." Jack extended his hand to Jeff, and then left the bar.

Jeff had only just enough time to make it to the airport for his flight, so he paid his tab and left Wahlberg for the airport in New York. He felt he had been living in a dream. How could Annie possibly have been so involved in the situation that she had to lose her life? He wondered at her dedication to her brother, and her sense of needing to protect him. He felt very angry toward Marty, yet somewhat compassionate for the situation he had gotten himself into. Fleeting images of people from the eyes of a child flashed through his mind. How would he find Laurie Cameron? Where would she be?

Jeff arrived at the airport, got his boarding pass, and passed through the security check-point. Before he arrived at his gate for his flight, he called Don Ribold.

"Hi, Don. It's Jeff Lipton. Just wanted to check to be sure you are still expecting me tomorrow morning."

Don greeted Jeff and assured him that he had pulled together some things to share with Jeff when he arrived. He also mentioned that Sophie was planning to fix them a light lunch.

"I'll drive over as soon as I pick up my cat from the vet and return her to my apartment." Jeff wanted to tell

Don about his visit with Jack Jenkins, but decided that some of the secrets may have to remain secrets, as far as Don was concerned. "I'll see you late tomorrow morning."

Jeff hung up the phone and walked to his gate to board his plane flight back to Aubrey. He felt frustrated and agitated at the whole scenario he had uncovered in Wahlberg. So much there seemed somewhat familiar to him, yet seemed to be part of a dream rather than reality. Did Annie know she was dying? Was Jack still covering up something that he hadn't told Jeff? He knew who Laurie was, but he had managed to wiggle out of any comments on her whereabouts. He must have known about the adoption if he was so close to Annie. And what did Don know? He would find that out tomorrow. He leaned back in his seat and stared out at the clouds below the plane.

By the time the plane landed, it was already 8:30. He carried his bag to his car and drove to his apartment. Since he hadn't talked to his parents for a couple of days, he decided to give them a quick call.

"Hi, Dad. It's kind of late, but I wanted to just check in with you. I've been in New York for the last couple of days, attending a seminar for the dealership. I'm going to Chatsworth in the morning, so won't get a chance to stop by until sometime Sunday, more than likely."

"Ok, Jeff. Thanks for letting us know what you are up to. Bye." George hung up the phone, and walked back into his family room, where Sue was watching television. "Jeff's back in town, but he's going to see Don Ribold tomorrow. He said he'd stop by sometime on Sunday."

Sue watched him sit down in the recliner, and returned to watching the program without comment.

Jeff walked to the kitchen to get a beer out of the refrigerator, when the phone rang.

"Hello?"

"Hi, Jeff. It's Carol. Just checking on you. Are we still on for tomorrow night?"

"Hi! Yes we are still on for tomorrow night. I'll call you from Chatsworth at the Ribolds'. I have so much to tell you about, and you won't believe it all. I'm looking forward to seeing you tomorrow." Jeff was smiling as he thought of Carol.

"Great! I'll see you then. Bye!" She hung up the phone, with Jeff still hanging on the line.

"Bye," he said, shaking his head as he hung up. *What a woman!* He was looking forward to seeing Carol, and he felt a stirring as he thought about her.

When Jeff awoke the next morning it was already near 8 o'clock. He put on some sweats and running shoes and went for a run to clear his head and get his blood pumping. After a quick shower and a bowl of cereal, he drove to the vet's to get Molly, who was more than happy to get out of her temporary quarters. She scolded him on the way back to the apartment for leaving her with strangers. With Molly back in place, and her food set out for her, Jeff started out for Chatsworth for his meeting with Don Ribold.

"Jeff, good to see you again," Don extended his right hand to shake hands with Jeff. "Come on in to the kitchen." He motioned for Jeff to follow him, so Jeff stepped into the foyer and closed the door behind him.

The house felt warm and welcoming. Coffee was brewing on the kitchen counter, and the table was covered with an assortment of papers and photographs. Don motioned for Jeff to sit down at the far side of the table, and took a seat closer to the counters.

"I've been digging through all these pictures and albums since you were here last week. It's been fun to reminisce about my beautiful Annie. She was beautiful, you know!" Don smiled at Jeff.

"So I've observed from her pictures. I have also learned that you were summoned to New York when Annie was in the hospital. Can you tell me about that, Don?"

"I'll get to that. But first I want to show you some of these albums from when Annie was a kid. You are welcome to take some of these if you like. I think Annie would want you to have them." Don put his reading glasses on, and reached for the first album. "Can I get you a cup of coffee before we start?"

"Sure. But I can get it." Jeff stood up and walked to the counter where the coffee pot had finished brewing and poured coffee into one of the waiting cups. "Can I get a cup for you?"

"No, I've had plenty. But thanks."

Jeff added a bit of sugar and some cream to the strong brew, and returned to the table. For the next hour they poured through pictures of Annie growing up. There were pictures of Marty as well, and snapshots that included Don and Arlene. Jeff admired the handsome family. From looking at the pictures, there was no indication of any friction in the family.

When they got to pictures of Annie's prom, Don told Jeff only that this was the beginning of some troubles with Annie. "Without going into any detail, I can tell you that prom night for Annie turned out to be a turning point in our relationship. We found out that she had gotten herself mixed up with the wrong crowd, and there didn't seem to be a turning back for Annie after that. She went away to college, and seemed to become a totally different person. It was very hard on your grandmother and me." Don shook his head to indicate his helplessness in the situation. "But we never stopped loving her, Jeff."

"I'm sure you didn't. Do you have pictures of her from college?"

"Hardly any. She came home for the holidays that year; Thanksgiving, Christmas, and Easter. Then at the end of the school year, she ran off with your father,

Mark Moss. We didn't hear from her again until about six years later." Then he related his story to Jeff.

Don and Arlene had just sat down to dinner when the phone rang. They looked at each other to see who was going to go for the phone first, and Don pushed back his chair to walk back out to the kitchen. Both had put in a long day at work.

"Hello?" Don answered, waiting for the response.

"Is this Don Ribold?" the voice on the other end of the phone asked.

"Yes it is."

"This is Jack Jenkins. I'm with the Wahlberg, New York Police department. Your daughter, Annie Moss, is hospitalized here in Wahlberg, and she has asked that we notify you."

"Annie? Is she seriously ill?"

"I'm afraid she is, sir. She has had some extensive surgery, and her condition is very grave. I would recommend that you come here as soon as possible. I'm really sorry to have to call you with this news."

"We will, Mr. Jenkins, Detective Jenkins, is it? How can I get in touch with you? I'll call the airlines as soon as we get off the phone, and I'll call you back to let you know when we will be arriving there. Where did you say? Wahlberg, New York? Is there an airport there?"

Don grabbed a pencil and the back of an old envelope to write on.

"That's right, W-a-h-l-b-e-r-g. There is a regional airport here, so you should be able to get a hop from New York, or you can rent a car and drive it. It's only a fairly short drive out of the city. My phone number is (909)112-5555."

"That might be a good plan. We'll fly into New York and rent a car. I'll get back in touch with you tonight." Don set down the phone, and grabbed the phone book.

"Annie is in the hospital in New York in serious condition. That was a policeman from Wahlberg, New York. He says Annie is asking for us." He flipped through the yellow pages in the phone book to find the airlines numbers.

Arlene jumped up from her chair to join him at the table, and helped him get to the right page for the airlines. She dialed the number, and Don talked to the ticket agent to arrange the flight. They could leave tonight on a late flight out that would get them to New York in the early hours of the morning. Arlene looked up the phone number for the rental car company, and they reserved a car from the airport as well. While Don returned a call to Jack, Arlene ran up to the bedroom to throw together clothes for the trip. They were out the door within an hour and on their way to the airport to see the daughter they had not seen in six years.

The flight was smooth and on time; the car was ready and waiting for them, and the attendant provided them with a map and instructions for getting out of the city to Wahlberg. Jack had provided directions to the hospital from the highway.

When they arrived at the hospital, the hallways were very quiet, except for the emergency room. They took the elevator to the third floor and walked quickly to the nurses' station. A nurse was on duty, watching monitors from the various rooms under her care.

"My name is Don Ribold. My wife and I are here to see Annie Moss." Don's hands were trembling at the prospect of seeing his daughter. He noticed that Arlene looked very tired, and her eyes were moist with tears.

"Yes, Ms. Moss is in Room 372. I have instructions to allow you both to go in to see her when you arrive. Please be careful not to excite or alarm her, as her condition is very tentative. I'll be right here if you need me."

The nurse pointed out the direction in the hallway to Annie's room. When they opened the door to see Annie, both were alarmed at the equipment that surrounded her. Annie's dark hair framed her face on the pillow, as she lay sleeping.

Arlene took her hand. "Annie, we're here. We came as quickly as we could." Tears streamed down her face as she spoke to her daughter. She patted Annie's hand.

Slowly, Annie opened her eyes. "Hi, Mom, Dad. I'm glad you came. There are so many things I want to say to you." Annie's voice was trembling.

"Not now, sweetie," said Arlene. "We'll be right here beside you, and all that can wait."

Don reached out to lay his hand on her shoulder. "We love you, Annie. Everything is going to be okay." He choked with the last of his sentence. The monitors beeped and whirred as they tracked Annie's vital signs. The IV dripped its solution into her veins.

Annie closed her eyes again. "I love you, too. And I'm so sorry," she whispered. "I've been away so long, and I've missed you."

Don and Arlene watched their daughter, noting any change in the monitors. Nurses came and went, making notes on charts and graphs. Both nodded off in the chairs a few minutes at a time, being exhausted from the trip and the lack of sleep. Early the next morning, a nurse came in to ask them to step out to the nurses' station, as Jack Jenkins has asked for them. They could return to Annie's bedside in a few minutes.

"I'm Jack Jenkins," said Jack, as he greeted Don and Arlene. "I'm sure you are wondering what has happened to Annie. Annie is a very brave young woman. At her request, she was helping us to apprehend some drug dealers here in Wahlberg, and unfortunately took a bullet intended for me. I can't tell you how devastated I am by all this. Annie is a very good friend as well. The doctors say that the bullet hit her carotid artery. They have done some extensive repairs, but there are still many things that could go wrong. Is there anything I can do for you?"

"I don't understand. You put my daughter in a dangerous situation without protection? Annie is not a police officer, is she?" Don was immediately angry with Jack.

"No, sir, she is not. Annie's a very strong-willed person. She knew about our plans to smoke out these drug dealers, and she insisted on helping us, mostly because of her husband Mark and his untimely death. We thought we had everything covered, but we underestimated the situation." Jack could hardly look at Don as he explained. Nervously, Jack shifted from his left to his right foot, studying the pattern in the floor.

"Right now all I'm concerned about is Annie's recovery. Arlene, we need to get back in to be with her, in case she wakes up again. Officer Jenkins, I'm sure we will be talking again later. The nurses tell us that you saved Annie's life by staying with her until she could get in here to the operating room. Thank you for that." Don put his hand on Jack's shoulder. "I'm sure this isn't easy for you either."

Arlene started back down the hall for Annie's room without a word to Jack. A flood of emotions took hold of her as she hurried back to the room. She was so glad that Annie had called for them, but why had she not contacted them before this? Why had she waited so long, and until she was so gravely injured, before she reached out to them? All of it didn't matter at all to her at that moment.

As she entered the room, the nurses were scrambling to get equipment to Annie's bedside.

"What's wrong?" Arlene asked.

"Ma'am, you'll have to stay back. The patient's blood pressure has spiked and she has developed a leak in her incision. The doctor is on his way. Please wait outside."

Arlene backed away from the scene, and took hold of the door handle, just as the doctor came rushing inside. Stepping out into the hall, Arlene met Don coming toward the door.

"Something's gone wrong. The nurses have gathered around Annie, and the doctor has been called back." Arlene fell into Don's arms. "Don, we can't lose her now, after all this time."

"Hold on, Arlene. It may be just an adjustment the doctor has to make to her medicine or something."

Jack was aware of the commotion outside Annie's room, and ran down the hallway. "What's going on?"

"Arlene said the nurses chased her out of the room, and the doctor has been called in. We don't know what is happening." Don looked at Jack with fear in his eyes.

The doctor came out of Annie's room. Jack immediately introduced him to the Ribolds.

"Mr. and Mrs. Ribold, we did everything we could to save Ms. Moss, but I'm afraid we have lost her. Her blood pressure rose too fast for the incision to hold, and she has hemorrhaged from her carotid artery. I'm so sorry for your loss. She was a beautiful young woman." The doctor then turned to Jack. "Jack, sorry we couldn't do more for her. If you need anything from me, just let me know."

He turned and walked away from the three of them, removing his face mask and his hat, and wiping his brow with his arm. Don, Arlene, and Jack stood silently, except for the soft sobs as Arlene buried her face in Don's jacket. Don noted the tears in Jack's eyes, and knew that the young man was indeed a good friend to Annie, and maybe more.

"I'll work on making the arrangements for Annie," Don said finally. "Jack, can you put me in touch with a funeral home here in Wahlberg. I'm sure they can make the arrangements to transport Annie back to Green Meadow."

Jack looked at Don. "There will have to be an autopsy, due to the circumstances of her death. That will take an extra day. If you can come to my office, I'll give you all the information you need. Don and Arlene, I can't tell you how sorry I am. Losing Annie puts a huge void in my life."

A nurse emerged from Annie's room. "If you would like to see your daughter for just a moment before we move her, you are welcome to go in now. I'll be back shortly." The nurse walked on down the hallway toward the nurses' station.

Jack stood outside while Don and Arlene went back in to see Annie. All of the equipment had been removed, and she lay as though she were sleeping on the pillow, her long, dark hair smoothed out to frame her face. She looked pale from her affliction, but serene in her death.

"Don, if only she had contacted us before this. We could have had so many good times together. She's all grown up now, but she's gone." Arlene choked as she tried to talk.

Don put his arm around her shoulder. "Arlene, she's at peace now. Whatever her life had become, she has put it all behind her. She will always be our little girl. We'll take her home to bury her in Green Meadow, where we can visit her and cherish our memories of her. Let's go now, and we'll get some rest before we go back." He pulled her to him, then ushered her back out into the hallway of the hospital. Jack walked with them to the hospital doorways, and then explained how to get to his office.

"When we get to the office, we'll call and get you a room to get some sleep. I'll make the arrangements through the police department. If there is anything else I can do, please call on me." Jack walked to his own car and drove to the police station with the Ribolds close behind him. Annie. How would he ever deal with the pain he was feeling? He had so many hopes for the future. Annie had indicated that there might be a chance for them, and he was sure of it. Now all that was gone, and he felt a sickening guilt in the pit of his stomach. If he had done just one part of the setup differently, would Annie be alive yet today? He knew that the question would never be answered, but that he would be haunted by it for the rest of his life.

Don finished telling Jeff the story of their trip to New York to see Annie, and then to bring her back with them to Green Meadow for the burial. His voice stammered slightly as he showed Jeff the last small album of pictures he had taken at the visitation and the funeral. "You should have all of these now, Jeff," he said as he closed the bindings.

Jeff took the album and laid it on the corner of the table. Sophie set up some soup and sandwiches on the patio for them, since the table was covered with pictures and albums. As they ate lunch together, Don shared more about Annie as a child and growing up in Green Meadow. Don was also very interested in what Jeff was doing with his life in Aubrey, and was curious about the adoptive parents.

"How was it that Arlene and I didn't know about you when Annie was in the hospital?"

"From what Captain Jenkins told me, Annie's friend Laurie had gone in to see her while Jack was away from the hospital. All of the friends were sworn to secrecy about me evidently, and all honored Annie's wishes by not telling you about my existence. What's missing for me is this friend, Laurie Cameron. I found out when I was in New York that Laurie Cameron left the bank at the same time that Annie died, but she left no forwarding address. Jack was completely evasive about Laurie, so I am not sure if he knows about her or not. I need to find Laurie to complete the puzzle surrounding my adoption." Jack sat back in his chair and looked pensively at Don.

"So you think this Laurie knows the circumstances surrounding the adoption? Do you think Annie asked her to find your adoptive parents? If that's the case, how did they get the paperwork done so quickly that Annie could sign the papers before her death?" Don's curiosity was peaked.

"I'll do some more research when I get a chance to get to a library." Jeff finished his lunch. Sophie brought them refills on iced tea, and he and Don talked about Don's career.

"Tell me about Arlene," said Jeff.

"It took a long time for Arlene to come back from her mourning of Annie's death. She blamed herself for not trying harder to find Annie and make amends. We moved here from Green Meadow so she was closer to work at the paper plant, and I went to work for the insurance company office here in Chatsworth. Eventually, Arlene got back into her routine of work and home. She had always been active in the church, and she loved gardening. Then one day she found a lump in her breast and had it checked out. It was cancerous, and had already advanced and spread. She died about nine months later, after some really tough times at home and in the hospital." Don stood up and walked to the edge of the patio. "She was a wonderful wife and mother, Jeff. I'll never totally understand the rift between her and Annie."

"I'm sure that's true. But Arlene and Annie aren't the first mother and daughter to reach an impasse in their relationship." Jeff rose and walked to stand beside Don. "So tell me about Sophie."

Don smiled. "Sophie was a breath of fresh air in my widower life. Arlene had been gone for a while when I met up with Sophie. She walked into my life one day many years ago, then reappeared all of a sudden, and things haven't been the same since. I'll tell you all about it sometime. Isn't that right, Sophie?" Sophie walked out onto the patio, just as Don was finishing his comment to Jeff.

"And don't forget for a moment that my life is no longer normal either!" She poked fun at Don and laughed.

"You'll have to meet Marty one day soon. He took Annie's death really hard, and had some of his own problems after graduation from college. I think he's got his life together now, and seems really happy."

Jeff didn't raise any questions about Marty. If Don wasn't ready to share any of the history he knew about Marty's life, then it was best left unsaid at this point. He certainly didn't know how involved Marty had been in Annie's death.

"Jeff, it's been great to share with you this afternoon. I hope you and I can see each other often and catch up on the years that have slipped away from us. Do you play golf?"

Jeff smiled at him. "Grandpa, you have yourself a golf partner." He embraced Don briefly and pulled away from him. "George's parents live close by in Aubrey, so I have had grandparents to grow up with. Sue's parents live in New York City, and I don't see them very often, but they've always been good to me. I look forward to getting to know you." Jeff walked toward the table.

"Sophie, can I help you carry in some of these dishes?"

Sophie started to stack up the plates and utensils. "If you want to carry in a few things on your way out, that would be great. And you are welcome back any time, Jeff."

Jeff was soon on his way. He stopped to fill up with gas at the station where he and Carol had stopped on their first trip to Chatsworth. After paying for his gas and Coke, he stopped at the phone booth to call Carol. "I'm on my way out of town, so will see you shortly," he said, when she answered the phone.

"Great! I'll be waiting for you. And you can meet my mom!" Carol placed the phone in the charger and went to her bedroom to dress. What to wear? Jeff said they were going to go out to dinner, and then to a movie. She wanted to look her best for him tonight, but not overdressed. She guessed he would be pretty casual, since he had been visiting with his grandfather. She laid out a pair of khaki slacks and a blouse, and then grabbed a bra and panties and headed for the shower. She had just enough time to bathe and dress before Jeff arrived.

Chapter 21
JEFF AND CAROL

By the time Jeff arrived at Carol's house, it was nearly 5:30. Carol lived in a modest neighborhood in Green Meadow. The streets were newly paved and curbed, and it appeared that many of the homeowners had put in new driveways while the street work had been done. A huge ash tree and an oak tree stood in the front yard, framing the house, wrapped in mostly brick with some siding on the gabled ends. Mums were still blooming around the porch, but were mostly covered with leaves that had fallen from the ash tree. The oak tree had yet to turn colors for fall. Daylight was already fading. A porch light was turned on in anticipation of the visitor.

Jeff walked to the front door and rang the bell. Carol came to the door almost immediately. "Hi, Jeff. Come on in." She opened the door and let it swing open as she installed her earring in her right ear lobe. "My mom's in the kitchen, and she's anxious to meet you." She gave him a quick peck on the cheek. "I told her you were tall, dark and handsome!" She laughed and her eyes sparkled with mischief.

Jeff followed her to the kitchen. "Mom, this is Jeff. Jeff, this is my mother, Jolene Braun." Carol turned from one to the other as she introduced them, still wearing her radiant smile.

"I'm so happy to meet you, Mrs. Braun. Carol has told me so much about you. And by the way, congratulations on your recent news." Jeff extended his hand and took hers.

"Well, thank you, Jeff. Please call me Jolene. Carol has been here for me all during my illness, and she has been a rock. Now maybe she can get on with her life." Jolene smiled, and Jeff could see where Carol had gotten her radiance.

Carol took her jacket from the back of a chair in the kitchen. "Jeff, I checked the paper, and we have just enough time to get to the next show, if you want to see a movie tonight."

"Okay. Good to meet you, Jolene. Sorry we have to run." Jeff followed Carol out of the kitchen and to the front door, reaching ahead of her to open the door on their way out. He provided the same courtesy when they reached the car.

"Wow, I can get used to this!" Carol teased, as she got into the passenger side of the front seat.

Jeff walked around the car and, taking the wheel, pulled away from the curb. "Tell me which way I need to go, and what we are going to see," he said.

"There are several good movies out right now. We can go to the theater complex, and decide which one to see when we get there."

They drove to the cinema, agreed on a film and bought their tickets. Carol picked up some popcorn and drinks.

"I can't wait to tell you about the last several days," Jeff said to her as they were waiting for the movie to begin. "You won't believe what I have learned. But there are still some missing pieces. Maybe you can help me out with them." He smiled at her as she munched on the popcorn.

They watched the film, and enjoyed the romantic comedy they had selected. After the movie was over, they walked back to the car. Jeff took her hand as they walked.

"There's a great place to eat I'd like to take you to in Aubrey, but it would be pretty late by the time we finish dinner. We may have consumed some alcohol. Would you be up for spending the night at my apartment? I'm willing to sleep on the couch." He winked at her and smiled.

Carol looked into his eyes. "Jeff Lipton, you are a very devious person. But I'll take the couch!" She punched him in the arm, and they were quickly on their way to Aubrey.

On their way, Jeff told her all about his meeting with Jack Jenkins, what he had found out at the bank, and his meeting that day with Don Ribold. Carol listened with total attention. She sensed that Jeff was still frustrated with those haunting questions.

"So you still don't know about how the adoption really came about? Maybe your parents are someone that this Laurie knew, who were looking for a child. Or maybe one of her other friends knew of your folks? There has to be a way to find Laurie Cameron. I say we go to the library tomorrow, and we'll do some searching. My guess is that there is a record somewhere on what happened to Laurie Cameron of Wahlberg, New York."

Carol's support and enthusiasm continued to overwhelm Jeff. He had never known anyone so spontaneous and self-assured. As he glanced at her, he noted the highlights of her blond hair as the headlights of cars they met shone through the windshield. He reached out to take her hand as he drove the remainder of the distance to Aubrey.

Jeff drove up to the front of the Country Club and was met by the attendant.

"Hello, Mr. Lipton. Are you dining with us tonight?"

"Yes, I am, thanks," Jeff responded.

The attendant tore off a claim ticket and handed it to Jeff. "You can leave the keys in the car, and I'll park it for you. Here's your claim ticket, which you can present to the maitre de when you are ready to leave. Have a great evening."

Jeff got out of the car, and walked around to the passenger side to open the door for Carol.

"I don't know if I'm dressed up enough to eat here," she said, as she stepped out of the car.

"Don't let the valet parking fool you. The dining is really very casual inside, and the food is outstanding. We often bring customers here, and our annual Christmas party is held here. Would you like to be my guest this year?" Jeff held her hand as they walked up the steps to the front door.

"I'd be honored, Mr. Lipton," Carol answered, curtsying slightly to Jeff.

They walked to the entrance to the dining room, and were met by the maitre de, who led them immediately to a table near the windows. From their perspective they could see the lights reflecting on the water in the lake below the windows. Music played in the background, and the tables were set with linens and china.

The waiter arrived to greet them. "My name is Joseph, and I'll be your waiter this evening. Can I get you something to drink to get you started?"

Carol ordered a glass of wine, and Jeff ordered a martini. He also asked that Joseph bring them some of the stuffed mushrooms, a house specialty. "Certainly, sir, these will be right out."

Joseph left them to get their order, and they each picked up a menu to decide on a meal.

"Whew, Jeff, these are kind of expensive!" Carol exclaimed, as she reviewed the entrees on the menu.

"Only the best for a very special lady," he replied, smiling at Carol. He reached for her hand, grasping it.

Carol blushed and looked down at the menu again. "What do you recommend?" She did not pull her hand away, but rather enjoyed Jeff's touch.

"If you'd like for me to order for us, I'll be glad to do that. Everything on the menu here is outstanding. Do you prefer meat, fish or fowl?"

"I think I'm in the mood for a good steak. I like it sort of medium, pink but not bloody. And I'd prefer a salad with whatever the house dressing might be. I suspect it's really good." She noted each of the items with her hands, as she described her request to Jeff.

Jeff laughed at her animation. When Joseph returned with their drinks and the appetizer, he released her hand to let her eat. Jeff placed their orders, handed over the menus and they made a toast to their new relationship.

By the time the dinner was completed and they had enjoyed several drinks and conversation, they had spent three hours in the Country Club. They talked about past relationships, career goals, and college experiences, but not much about Jeff's quest to find out about his mother.

Joseph finally brought them the check. "Is there anything else I can get for you?" he asked.

"No, Joseph. Everything was wonderful." Jeff got out his credit card and placed it on the tray for Joseph. "If you'll take care of this, and order my car for me, we'll be on our way." Jeff also handed him the claim check for his car.

As they left the Country Club, Jeff held Carol's hand as they walked down the steps to the car. As he opened the car door, Carol turned to kiss him.

"This has been a wonderful evening, Jeff. Thank you so much." The kiss was light, her lips moist. Jeff put his arm around her and pulled her closer to him. He kissed her again, this time with more pressure, his lips slightly parted.

"It's been my pleasure, Carol." He released her and closed the door after her.

They drove to Jeff's apartment, exchanging small talk, each lost in thoughts of what might develop when they got inside his apartment. The messages in the kisses had been unmistakable to both of them.

Jeff looped his arm into Carol's as they walked up the steps to his apartment. When Jeff unlocked the door, they were greeted by Molly, anxious to see Jeff after spending the day in the apartment alone.

"Oh, Jeff, she's beautiful!" Carol exclaimed.

"Molly, meet Carol," Jeff laughed at Molly's attention to Carol as he closed the door behind them. He was glad for Molly's appearance to relieve the tension that had settled between them.

"Carol, can I fix you a drink?"

Carol placed her purse on the kitchen table, and glanced around the apartment. "If you have a glass of wine, I'll take one. If not, I can drink a beer." She was pleased at the appearance of the apartment. Although it had a certain bachelor pad quality, it was nicely decorated with just the necessities in furniture. Artwork around the living room reflected Jeff's interest in landscapes. A few still life paintings in small frames were strategically placed around the kitchen. The leather couch and recliner looked warm and welcoming. Carol took a seat on the couch, waiting for Jeff to bring her drink.

"I think I can sleep on this," she smiled at Jeff as he came from the kitchen.

He sat down beside her, handing her a glass of wine. She took the glass, and took a sip, setting it on the coffee table.

Jeff got up and walked over to the music center. "What kind of music do you like? I have rock, jazz, and even some long-hair that I got from my mom."

"Oh, I love Jazz. You pick one out."

Jeff placed two CDs in the tower and set the sound system to his liking. Then he walked back over to sit with Carol on the couch. He felt completely relaxed with Carol, although not quite sure at the moment just how far things might go tonight. He put his arm around her and pulled her shoulder into his side. Her hair brushed his cheek, and he could smell the subtle scent of her perfume. She seemed a little tense in his arms, and he sensed that she was also unsure of their relationship. The music was soothing, and they listened for a few moments in silence.

"Jeff, you haven't told me how you feel about your mother, now that you have found out more about her." Carol had pulled away from him and sat facing him on the couch, her legs tucked up under her on the cushion.

He smiled at her, and picked up his beer off the coffee table. "I think I'm beginning to understand more about her. She was obviously devoted to my father. It also appears that she wanted to do what was best for me, knowing that she was dying. What I still don't understand is why she would choose strangers to raise me over my grandparents. Don seems like such a good guy, and I didn't get to know him when I was growing up. I'm hoping that if and when I find Laurie Cameron, I will also find some answers for that question as well. What do you think?"

Carol set her wine glass on the coaster and leaned forward to kiss him. "I think Annie knew exactly what she was doing. She loved you and wanted you to be with people who would love you and give you everything that she was not going to be able to give you. That's an incredible sacrifice of love in my book."

Jeff thought about Carol's comment for a moment, watching her blue eyes as she talked about Annie.

"Carol, you have brought so much joy into my life these last couple of weeks. You are so intuitive and smart, and you have a way of looking at things with perfect vision." He set his beer down, and took her hands in his. "Beside that, you are a very beautiful woman." He pulled her toward him, and kissed her. She did not pull away from him.

Jeff stood up and pulled her to her feet and took her in his arms. With slow movements, and in time with the music, they danced to the CD. The kisses become more intense and the contact of their bodies aroused them physically.

Jeff pulled away far enough to be able to unbutton the buttons on Carol's blouse. Slowly, he pushed the fabric off her shoulder, as he continued to dance with her, exposing her bra. She let the blouse fall away from her arm, and slipped the other arm out as well.

Carol raised the bottom of Jeff's sweater to ease it up and over his shoulders, and then helped him slip it off over his head. His T-shirt was next, easily discarded on top the sweater on the recliner.

With one swift movement, Jeff had unhooked her bra, and pulled her close to him, feeling her breasts against his bare chest. She felt the prickle of his chest hair against her nipples, sending shocks through her body, as he began to move her toward his bedroom.

"So, let me get this straight. Neither of us is going to sleep on the couch tonight?" she asked between his kisses, teasing him as they moved through the bedroom door.

Jeff chuckled. "This is your last chance to make a break for it."

Their love making was intense and passionate, leaving both of them sated. The music continued to play as they fell asleep in each others arms.

Jeff awoke the next morning to the aroma of bacon and brewing coffee. Carol had already showered and wore his robe as she prepared some breakfast in the kitchen.

"Wake up!" she said as she poked her head into the bedroom. "Breakfast in 15 minutes!"

Jeff threw a pillow at her and moaned. "What time is it, anyway?" He rolled over to look at the clock and saw that it was already 9 AM. "I can't believe I slept this late," he said as he swung his legs out of bed and ducked into an old sweatshirt. "I'm famished!"

He walked into the kitchen and grabbed Carol around the waist. "How was the couch last night?" he chided.

She turned around and kissed him. "It was marvelous! Can I stay again tonight?" She turned back to the stove to flip over the bacon, and began placing it on the paper towels to drain.

"What! Can't get enough?" Jeff brought two plates over to the stove for the eggs and bacon, and patted her on the butt.

"Go sit down at the table. I'll not have my breakfast getting cold. Better yet, how about putting some bread in the toaster?" Carol nodded in the direction of the toaster as she gave him the directions.

Jeff put some bread in the toaster, and then walked to the door to the apartment to see if the paper was outside the door. He retrieved the paper in time to get back to the toaster to butter the toast. Together they brought all the breakfast items to the table. He watched her walking across the kitchen in his bathrobe and felt himself become aroused.

Carol poured some orange juice and coffee for each of them before she sat down. She kissed Jeff before she sat down, and he reached inside the robe to find that she had nothing on underneath. He stroked her body as he held her close to him. There was no turning back. Within a couple of minutes they were on the couch, again making love with unbridled passion, hungry for the newness of each others' bodies.

When they finally returned to the table, they laughed at the cold eggs and toast, but ate them hungrily. Molly sat near by, hoping for someone to drop a morsel of their breakfast for her to nibble. She walked to the table and rubbed against Carol's leg to get her attention.

"So, Molly, what do you think of this guy? Is he safe to be with?" Carol winked at Jeff and smiled.

"Now don't you girls start ganging up on me," Jeff was reading the paper and drinking his coffee. "Hey, Carol, there's an article here in the paper about a new resource in the library. It's designed to be able to do research on just about any subject. Do you think it might lead us to the whereabouts of Laurie Cameron?"

"Might be! Is the library open today?" Carol picked up their plates and carried them to the sink.

"It opens at one this afternoon. What can we do to pass the time until then?" He looked over the paper at her and grinned.

Carol threw a kitchen towel at him. "Well, we could go for a drive around Aubrey. You could show me where you work, where your parents live, and where you went to school."

Jeff gave a sigh of disappointment. "That's not what I had in mind, but if you insist."

They cleaned up the kitchen, showered and dressed. Jeff drove Carol around town to show her the sights of Aubrey, and then to a little diner, where Jeff often went for lunch on work days. He thought Carol would find it enjoyable, as the patrons were very similar to those he had met in Green Meadow at Peggy's Diner.

At one o'clock they went to the library. With some short instruction from the library aide and following the directions with the computer, they began to do word searches on Laurie Cameron. They looked within the context of the bank where she and Annie had worked. They looked within the city of Wahlberg. Jeff couldn't remember the name of the county where Wahlberg was located, but they found the county on a map search.

Through the county site, they searched for newspapers and periodicals in that area, and then finally searched again on Laurie Cameron's name, hoping for some link to a newspaper or magazine article.

Jeff's heart skipped a beat as he looked at the screen in disbelief. The county court listings indicated marriage licenses issued. Laurie Sue Cameron was married to George Keith Lipton on the day before Annie's death. Keith was the name of Laurie's friend who was with her at the hospital. Sue and George, his parents, were Laurie and Keith!

Jeff fumbled with his billfold to find the card that Jack Jenkins had handed him when he left the bar. He walked quickly to a pay phone near the entrance to the library, inserted the coins, and dialed the number.

"Blue Goose Bar," the voice answered.

"Is this Fred?" Jeff asked.

"Yes, who's this?"

"It's Jeff Lipton. I was in the bar on Friday talking to Jack Jenkins. Would you answer a question for me?"

"That depends. What is it?" Fred was apprehensive.

"Who was the owner of the bar when Jack bought it?" Jeff knew he was on the edge of full discovery.

"Keith somebody. Keith Liston or Lincoln. Lipton, that's it, Keith Lipton. Why do you want to know?"

"Thanks, Fred. You've answered my question." Jeff hung up the phone and walked back over to Carol. He sat down and stared at the computer screen.

"Jeff, are you okay?" Carol was alarmed at Jeff's expression.

"Let's go back to the apartment. I need some time to think," Jeff said, as he took her hand and logged out of the computer screen.

They drove back to Jeff's apartment in silence. Carol had seen the names and put the pieces together to know that Jeff's adoptive parents were more than just strangers who had adopted him as a child. They were Annie's friends. She also understood Jeff's state of mind, trying to make sense of all the secrecy surrounding Annie's death and the adoption.

When they got back to the apartment, Carol busied herself around the apartment to give Jeff some time to himself. Molly jumped up and curled in his lap as he sat in the recliner, stretching and purring against her master. Carol thought the animal was probably bringing some comfort to Jeff.

Finally, Jeff got up out of the recliner, sending Molly away, and walked over to the couch.

"Carol, come here and sit with me, will you?" he asked.

She didn't hesitate, but quickly walked to the couch to sit beside him. "Can I get you something to drink?"

"No, just sit here with me for a few minutes. I need to talk." Jeff took her hand in his. His hand was trembling slightly, and felt cold and clammy in hers. She clasped his hand between both of hers.

"Carol, I don't know what to do next. I have so many emotions going through me right now that I just don't know which way to turn. Thirty years of deceit, Carol!" Jeff sat forward on the couch. "My own parents have been hiding all this from me for thirty years. They not only knew who Annie was, they were her friends! What do I say to them? Do I just tell them that I know the truth? Should I give them a chance to come out with everything, since they know I've been to New York? My life and Annie's have been one long secret." Jeff leaned back again on the sofa, still holding Carol's hand.

"I'm sorry this is hurting you, Jeff. Would it help to look at the motivation for each of the people who have been involved?"

"What do you mean?"

"Well, let's start with Annie. Annie wanted you to be with people she trusted and was comfortable with. She hadn't seen your parents for six years, and they didn't know you. She knew she was dying and didn't have the time to make any introductions, and she evidently trusted Sue... er, Laurie."

"Yeah, yeah, go on."

"Don didn't know about you. He just was happy to have his daughter back and buried her in Green Meadow cemetery. Jack kept the secret because he was probably in love with Annie. Plus Jack had other reasons to keep things low key when the accident happened. When he heard your name was Lipton, he knew right away who your parents were."

"That explains Jack's reaction when I met him. When I told him my name, I knew there was something strange about his reaction. Now I know why." Jeff had cupped his hand on his chin, thinking through the scenarios Carol was presenting.

"George and Sue were probably sworn to secrecy by Annie. They may have agreed to keep all this a secret until you were old enough to be able to understand the whole picture. Jeff, I don't think anyone wanted to hurt you. I'd say everyone was trying to protect you. From what you have told me, George and Sue have been involved in your life since you were born." Carol held both of his hands now, and was sitting on the coffee table in front of him, looking into his eyes.

Jeff studied her for a moment. "You really are beautiful, you know. Inside and out. Thanks for helping me think through this. I still don't know what to do about my folks, though. Should I just call and tell them I'm coming over, and then start the conversation when I get there?"

"Jeff, at this point, I'd guess that they are as unsure of how to tell you the whole story as you are to hear it from them. It's got to be really hard for them. But you need to do this alone. Can you take me home yet before you see them later tonight?" Carol stood up as though she was ready to leave.

"You're right. I'll call and let them know I'll be over there this evening. It's better if I do this alone." Jeff stood up and kissed her.

He walked to the phone and dialed. Sue answered the phone.

"Hi, Mom. I wondered if you might want some company tonight for supper."

"Oh, hi, Jeff. Sure, I have plenty of food. What time do you think you will be here?" Sue was glad to hear from him.

"It will probably be close to 4:30 or even 5 o'clock before I get there. I'll look forward to seeing you then. Love you. Bye."

Jeff placed the phone back on the charger, staring at it for a moment. Carol had put on her coat and picked up her purse. Jeff glanced up at her.

"Let's go, beautiful. I have a long evening ahead of me."

Chapter 22
JEFF, SUE AND GEORGE

"Hey, Mom. Smells good in here!" Jeff kissed Sue on the cheek. He opened the oven door out of habit. "What's for dinner?"

"I grilled some chops, so it's just in the oven to keep it hot until you got here. I'll get everything on the table, and you can tell us about your week." Sue carried a dish of mashed potatoes to the table in the dining room and returned to the kitchen.

As usual, there was a fresh flower arrangement on the table of fall mums, probably from her garden. The plates and flatware were arranged perfectly with seasonal napkins and water goblets. Jeff could smell the coffee brewing, its aroma filling the air with the scent of vanilla and coffee beans.

"I'll help you." Jeff took out a tray of ice and dropped a few cubes in each of the three glasses on the table.

Then he filled a pitcher with water and poured the glasses full over the ice.

"Hey there, how's my boy?" George came into the dining room as Jeff was finishing the last glass. He extended his hand to Jeff, and then pulled him against him to give him an affectionate squeeze of his shoulder.

"I'm good, but I have a lot to tell you. I was in New York the last couple of days, and I went to Wahlberg where Annie lived." Jeff wanted to blurt out all he knew, but was curious to see if what he shared with them would bring out their story.

"Let's eat first, if you don't mind," Sue said with authority, as she brought in the chops and wiped her hands on a hand towel.

They said grace and started in on their meal. Sue talked a bit about her own adventures with the garden club and their latest plantings. George told Jeff about a wood working project he was developing in the garage. As they finished eating, and Sue poured them each a cup of coffee, she sat down and looked at Jeff.

"Jeff, we knew you were in Wahlberg. Jack Jenkins called us when he was talking with you at the bar there." Sue looked at George.

"Jack called you? I don't understand." Her statement had caught Jeff off guard.

"It's such a long story, Jeff. Let me just say up front that your mother was a very private person. She was very protective of you, and she loved you very much.

We have respected her wishes that you not know about any of the things you have found out in the last couple of weeks, until you were old enough to uncover them on your own." There was pain in Sue's face as she talked. George continued.

"Your mother and I have loved you since you were born," George said, reaching to place his hand on Jeff's arm.

"Jeff, please be patient, and we'll go back to the beginning and tell you the truth about how you came to be our son." Sue took a sip of her coffee, and swallowed hard. "Jack told you about how your mother died, is that right?"

"Yes, he told me about Marty and how Annie had taken his place in a sting operation to capture some drug pushers in Wahlberg. He told me about how she was shot, and that she was in very poor condition in the hospital, when Laurie went in to talk to her there."

"Jeff, my name is Laurie Sue Cameron Lipton. Your mother and I were very good friends in Wahlberg. On the day of her accident, we were there at the hospital waiting for news of her surgery. She asked for me. She had already told me that day that if anything happened to her, I was to take care of you. When I went in to see her in the room, she was convinced that she would not live."

"Hi, Laurie," said Annie, opening her eyes only slightly to see her friend. "I'm not going to make it." Tears rolled down her cheeks.

"Sure you will, Annie. The doctors have hopes that everything will be okay, but you have to be calm and just work at getting better." Laurie held her friend's hand.

"I need to make sure that you will raise Jeff for me," said Annie weakly. "You and Keith are the only ones I trust with him. Jack is going to get in touch with my parents, so they will be coming here. I want to be sure that you have custody of Jeff before they arrive, and that they do not know about him. Will you take care of that for me?"

"Annie, please, you need to just rest and get well. Jeff needs you to take care of him yourself." Laurie was fearful of Annie's agitation.

"If I get better, we can tear up the papers. But in case I don't, I want to be sure all this is taken care of. Please, Laurie?" Annie looked at her with pleading eyes.

"I'll do whatever you want. Do you want to see Jeff? Should I bring him here?"

"Oh no, I don't want to scare him, and to have him see me like this. I know you love him as though he were your own, so it makes perfect sense that you should raise him. Will you just take care of that for me?" Her tears had become sobs of grief for parting with her son.

"I'll go to an attorney's office first thing tomorrow. In fact I know of someone I could probably call yet tonight to get things rolling. Annie, I love you. Please don't leave us." Laurie laid her head on Annie's side and cried with her. When she could see that Annie had fallen back to sleep, she slipped out of the room.

Keith was waiting for her when she walked back down the hall to the waiting room. He held her as she trembled with emotion.

"Annie wants us to get adoption papers drawn up for Jeff," she said as she pulled back from Keith to look into his face.

"Adoption papers? She's going to be alright, isn't she?" he asked.

"She doesn't think she is going to make it, and she wants me, or us, to raise Jeff. Jack is calling her parents, so she wants us to get this done before they arrive, so that they do not know about Jeff." It occurred to Laurie that the whole plan was surreal.

"I can call my attorney yet tonight," Keith said as he looked at his watch. "Let's go back to your apartment and pick up Jeff, and we can talk about all this there."

Keith and Laurie left the hospital for Laurie's apartment. They drove in silence, each lost in thoughts of how to make all this work out for Annie. When they arrived, with Jeff in tow, Keith tossed his keys on the kitchen table and picked up the phone.

"Jim, this is Keith Lipton. I need a favor. Laurie and I have been asked to adopt the son of a friend, who may be dying. Can you draw up the paperwork for this tomorrow morning for us?" Jack paused, listening to the man on the other end of the phone line. He paced back and forth on the kitchen floor, holding the phone to his ear.

"Okay. We will be down at your office around 10 tomorrow morning, and we can give you all the information you need at that time. Thanks, Jim, I really appreciate this." Keith placed the phone back on the cradle and turned to Laurie.

"Laurie, I know this isn't the most romantic scenario for a proposal, but will you marry me? We have a lot of differences, but I think we can make a good life together, and we could give Jeff a stable home." Keith rambled and shifted from one foot to the other as he looked at Laurie, his hands in his pockets.

"Keith, are you sure? I'm not sure I can give you the kind of relationship you are looking for. I do know that we have Jeff's best interests at heart, and if you are serious about this, I accept." She put her arms around his neck, and he held her.

Jeff tugged at his sleeve. "Keith, why is everyone crying?"

"Everyone is just happy, Jeff," said Keith. "If you can go pick out a book, I'll read you a story."

Jeff ran off to the guest room to rummage through some books Laurie kept there for him. They both knew that it would take him a while to find the one he wanted.

"Laurie, let's take Jeff and go back to Iowa. My parents would love to have Jeff around to spoil, and we could start a new life together there in Aubrey. It might be good for us to use our other names. George and Sue. How does that sound to you? George and Sue Lipton." Keith spread out his arms as though presenting a banner with their names emblazoned on the surface. "I can sell the bar, and we would have enough money to get established there. You can work at a bank or something, and I can get a job as well. We'll be normal Midwestern Americans."

Laurie looked at him in disbelief. "You're serious, aren't you? You really want to take Jeff and go to Iowa?"

"Yes, it would be perfect. I can start putting out some feelers to see who might be interested in buying the bar. But we have to get the marriage license first thing tomorrow and get married. Then the adoption papers will read correctly."

"I think it sounds wonderful, Keith.. er, George. But what if Annie does make it, and we don't have Jeff after all?"

"I say we cross that bridge when we come to it. But let's get all the plans in motion. It will bring Annie relief to know that things are taken care of, and that Jeff will have a good life with us. If Annie makes it, then we will just tear up the adoption papers, and maybe move to Iowa anyway. What do you say?"

Laurie couldn't help but feel a sense of exhilaration at the thought of starting over in a new place with Keith. At the same time, she felt incredible grief at the thought of losing her best friend. She said simply, "Okay." Just then, Jeff came bounding into the living room with his book and plopped himself on Keith's lap.

"Annie asked that I have adoption papers drawn up, granting you to me and George to raise you. Your father is George Keith Lipton. We had been seeing each other for some time before all this happened. We decided to get married and bring you back to Iowa where he was raised. Annie made us promise that we would not let her parents know about you. She wanted us to raise you, as we had known you since you were an infant. We already loved you as though you were our own child." By now Sue's voice was shaking and tears rolled down her cheeks.

"I can't believe this. You have known this all this time, and you haven't told me? Why?"

George stood up and paced the floor at the end of the table. "Jeff, it is such a difficult situation. If you can imagine, Annie was your mother's best friend. Sue, or Laurie as Annie knew her, was there for her when your dad was killed, stood by her when you were born, and took care of you when Annie was working or running an errand. Annie saw it as only natural that we take you, if she were not going to be able to do it. But the secrecy with her family was at her request. She signed the papers, so that when her parents arrived at the hospital, you would already be our son. We got married that next day, had the adoption papers written, and Annie signed them the following day, before her parents arrived in Wahlberg. She didn't want you to see her in the hospital. She asked only that when you asked about her that we give you pictures."

"Jeff, you uncovered things so quickly. I didn't know how to tell you all that we knew. Jack called on Friday and told us you were in Wahlberg, and I told him at that time that we would tell you the rest of the story when you got home." Sue took another sip of her coffee, studying Jeff.

"So that's why he insisted that I see you? It all makes sense now. And that's why he found a quick way out of the bar when we got to the part where you went in to see Annie." Jeff looked at Sue. He stood up, pushing his chair back from the table.

"I have actually had time to think about all this. I saw Don Ribold yesterday, and he told me his story about getting to Wahlberg to see Annie, and how she died that day."

Jeff rubbed the back of his neck. "Last night I had a date with the girl I met in Green Meadow, and we had a really nice evening. This morning we went to the library and did some research, and I found your marriage license. I wanted you to tell me your story before I let you know I knew who you were."

George and Sue looked at each other, and George reached for her hand. Jeff walked around the table to kiss Sue on the cheek.

"I just need some time now to think. Be patient with me, okay?"

"Jeff, before you go, I have an album I got out of the attic when Jack called Friday. It has pictures of you and Annie and me from when you were first born to just before she died. I want you to have them." Sue walked over to the sideboard to get the album. She handed it to Jeff. "I hope this will make things a little easier to understand." She looked into her son's eyes.

"But there is more. You remember the key that was in the envelope I gave you? The night your father died, Annie called me from the police station, and asked me to take some things out of her apartment. When we finally got around to opening them, I helped Annie put the contents into a lock box at the bank. The access was in her name and mine. After her death, I had your name put on the lock box, and I've been maintaining it all these years."

"Is it at the bank where the two of you worked? What's in it?" Jeff's curiosity was peaked.

"The box contains a large amount of cash. I have no idea how much. It was money that your father earned from all that drug business before he was killed. You can take the key now and discover the money they so carefully guarded to care for you. After Mark was killed, Annie refused to spend any of the money, living instead on her income. She intended it for you, Jeff."

Jeff took the album. "I'll call you later," he said, as he walked back through the kitchen, grabbing a couple of cookies on his way out the door.

George put his arm around Sue's shoulder. "It will be alright. He'll come around, Sue."

Jeff went back to his apartment and set the album on the table in the kitchen. He changed into an old pair of jeans and a sweater, and slipped into some mules. His mind was so full of all the events from the last couple of days, he just wanted to sit in the recliner for a few minutes and relax. Jack. Marty. Annie. Laurie, or Sue? Keith, or George? The characters were real. He went back through the accident as Jack had related it to him. He felt Annie's agony in hearing of Mark's death. He felt her pain as the bullet pierced her neck and she lay in surgery and intensive care. He felt Marty's grief and guilt in getting his sister involved. What about Sue and George? Did they get married just to adopt him, as Annie lay dying in the hospital?

He looked at the album lying on the table. He opened the cover. There on the first page of the album were pictures of Annie with a man that must have been Mark, his father. He noted the dark hair, pulled back to the base of his neck, and the similarity in the eyes to his own. He had one arm around Annie, and she had both arms looped around his waist. She looked very happy. Her long, straight hair hung over her shoulder, dark and shining in the sunlight.

The next several pages were of Annie and Sue in places probably around the city. Annie's profile was changing with the growth of the baby. There were a number of snapshots of Jeff as a newborn baby, in his mother's arms, in Sue's arms, in a bassinet, and in a stroller. Other pages chronicled the three of them as Jeff grew older. Each had a notation as to when and where it was taken, and indicated the people in the photos. Jack was in several of them, as were George and other friends. Jeff smiled as he looked at the pictures. He felt as though he knew all the characters in the photos, and felt a sense of warmth and belonging as he flipped through the pages a second time. He was convinced that Annie loved him. And he also knew that Sue loved him as well.

He finally closed the album and laid it carefully on the coffee table in his apartment. He took the key from his pocket and turned it as he inspected its flat surface. There would have to be another trip to New York scheduled sometime soon.

He flipped on the TV only to find that it was already 10 o'clock. Knowing that Carol was expecting him to call, he quickly dialed her number.

He smiled as he heard her voice on the other end of the line.

"Hello?"

"Hey there. Sorry to call you so late, but I knew you would be expecting to hear from me."

"No problem. How did things go?"

"George and Sue told me all about their relationship with Annie and the real story of my adoption. But I'll get into that with you later. I have a proposition for you." Jeff stood up and paced the length of the couch with the phone.

"What's that?"

"If I get us some tickets to a play in New York, will you go there with me next weekend?" Jeff wanted her by his side.

"Next weekend? Carol was laughing with Jeff. "Sure, I'll go, crazy man. Will there be a couch for me to sleep on?"

"Only if you can get away from me, and that's not likely to happen. I'll get back to you as soon as I know more about the time for our flights, but we'll plan on leaving on Friday after work. Carol, I think it's going to be a very special weekend."

Jeff hung up the phone and sat for a moment, only half listening to the news. Molly jumped up into his lap and curled against him, purring loudly.

"Molly girl, today's the first day of a new life for us."

EPILOGUE

Carol carried a plate of hamburger patties out the back door to Jeff, who was working with the flame on the grill. Jeff had on a chef's hat and an apron with his last name embroidered on the front. As Carol approached with the plate of uncooked meat, he stepped back to make room for her to set them on the table beside the grill.

"Thank you, Ma'am. I'll have these on the flame directly, and ready to eat before you know it!" He grinned at her, then kissed her on the cheek.

Carol smiled and walked back across the patio, weaving between chairs filled with guests.

"Can I help you bring out some of the food," asked Sophie, as she followed Carol to the door.

"Sure, Sophie, come on in." Carol held the door for her. The kitchen counter was full of a variety of dishes for the outdoor feast. Sophie had made a big bowl of potato salad, which she picked up and took outside, still wrapped with its cellophane wrapper. Carol handed her a large spoon to use for serving.

Just as Sophie walked out the door, Sue emerged from the living room, holding a small child in her arms.

"Looks like Annie woke up!" said Carol, as she kissed the baby girl on the cheek. "Or did Grandma just get tired of waiting to see her?" She grinned at Sue.

"Now would I do anything like that?" Sue rolled her eyes at Carol, and snuggled the baby close to her. "Little girls are something new for me, you know."

"And I've got the experience with the girls!" Carol's mother, Jolene, joined them in the kitchen. "All those men out there are talking baseball and race cars! How's our little girl doing?" She peaked at little Annie, as Sue held her on her shoulder.

"If one of you wants to put a bottle on, I'm sure she will be asking for it very soon," said Carol, as she pushed the door of the refrigerator shut with her foot and handed Jolene a bottle. She carried the mustard and ketchup to a tray she was preparing to take outside.

The doorbell rang, and Carol moved swiftly through the living room, wiping her hands on her hand towel. She opened the door to Marty, his wife, Janet and their two teenage boys.

"Marty and Janet, please come in, won't you?" Carol stood aside and motioned for them to walk into the foyer. "I know Jeff will be anxious to see you. The guys are mostly on the patio, and the gals are between there and the kitchen, as we get the food all ready to eat. You kids can go on out into the yard, if you like. Can I get you something to drink?"

"Thanks so much for getting us all together," said Marty. "We've been anxious to see little Annie again. Just show us the way to the drinks, and we can help ourselves."

"I brought a salad I thought everyone would enjoy," said Janet, handing Carol a colorful bowl filled with a fresh garden salad. They walked into the kitchen to join Jolene, Sue and Sophie.

"Oh, Carol, she is so beautiful!" said Janet, as she saw Annie, now hungrily nursing from her bottle in Sue's arms. Annie looked up and smiled at her, briefly releasing the nipple on the bottle to gurgles of formula. Janet put her finger in Annie's tiny hand. "Look, she can even grab my finger already."

Annie was content with all the attention from her Grandmothers, her great grandmother, and her great aunt Janet. She squirmed and wriggled, making room for the last drop of formula from the bottle. They passed her around, making baby noises, as Carol continued to set up the serving line on the patio.

Marty walked over to where Jeff was grilling the hamburgers. "How are things going for you, Jeff?" Marty asked, holding a can of Diet Coke in his left hand as he shook Jeff's hand with his right. Marty was still slight in build. He and Jeff had talked at length about his recovery from drug and alcohol abuse, his marriage to Janet, and his two boys. Marty had expressed to Jeff that Annie had saved his life. When she had died, he had been transformed by her sacrifice and had gotten the treatment he needed. His dad had helped him out financially while he got back on his feet, and he had been successful in finding a job in his field. He knew that Jack had told Jeff the whole story, but also knew that there was no reason for Jeff to tell Don about Marty's involvement at this point in his life. Jeff had reached a sense of forgiveness and understanding with Marty, and felt it was most important for him to feel a family unity.

"I'm good, Uncle Marty. Did you see my gorgeous little Annie when you came through the house?"

"Yes, I did. She looks just like Annie might have looked as a baby. Do you have pictures of our Annie as a baby?"

"Grandpa Don gave me some pictures some time ago, and Carol and I had them out one night to compare her baby pictures to little Annie. It's amazing how much she resembles her. We are glad for her to have Annie's name." Jeff beamed as he talked about his small daughter.

"By the way, I need to talk to you about a new car. Do you have time to drive down to the dealership sometime today after we eat? I have my eye on one in the lot." Marty would not have considered buying a car from anywhere but Jeff's company. And he knew that Jeff would give him a fair deal.

"Sure, we'll all take a drive over there later on. I want you to all see the new golf course that's almost ready as well. We need to get together for some golf this summer." Jeff made sure that Don and George heard him make the comment.

"You're on, Jeff," said Don. You youngsters think you can beat us old farts, but we'll show you a thing or two!" They all laughed at the thought of a foursome competing for the best score.

Within a few minutes, all the food was ready and the tables set for their cookout feast. Carol found a spot for Annie's car seat in the shade of the house, and handed her a ring of plastic keys to rattle. They all joined hands and sang a table prayer, then lined up for the buffet. There were the hamburgers, some with cheese, Sophie's potato salad, Janet's garden salad, Sue's green bean casserole, and several dishes that Carol had prepared, along with all the condiments for the burgers. There was soda and beer in the cooler, and each took his or her own selection from the ice.

As each settled into a spot at the tables, Jeff stood up and raised his glass. "To Annie's family," he said. The hodgepodge of family members all raised their glasses with Jeff and repeated after him, "To Annie's family!"

ABOUT THE AUTHOR

Linda Kay Christensen, a former farm girl from central Illinois, has enjoyed many years as a bank manager, a self-employed accountant and tax preparer (CPA), and an online instructor for Keller Graduate School (DeVry University). She earned her undergrad in Business Management and her Masters in Human Resources from the University of Illinois, Springfield. Linda's history in writing has included everything from business communication, teaching, and journaling to occasional poetry. Her inspiration for Annie's Love comes from a series of five prints by C. Clyde Squires given to her grandmother in 1916 as a wedding gift. The characters in these prints will come alive in Linda's series of the "five stages of love".

Linda helped her mother, Wilma Diekhoff, complete her memoirs in a book that includes 200 recipes from family and friends. Wilma held a book signing at Barnes and Noble at the age of 82. *Flavors From The Past* is now available in e-book format on Nook and Kindle. Linda is married to Jerry, a former engineer and now a master gardener, living in Fredericksburg, Texas. They have traveled extensively, meeting many characters who contribute to Linda's writing.